Reis has spent a year trying to keep the spirit of Anver-Kasyova alive, running Rainbow Bridge, a grassroots rescue network smuggling civilians out of war-torn Anver. It's all they and Edgar can do in the wake of the destruction of the cities' connecting bridge.

But when the Kasyovan Bureau arrests Reis, what should be the end turns into an unexpected new beginning: an invitation to lead the very country they've been fighting to save. Inducted into the Shadow Government, Reis becomes a reluctant President, aware they're a pawn, but powerless to say no. The Shadow Government has leverage...and a secret weapon: a powerful AI named Oracle, whose capability even surprises Edgar.

As Reis takes the helm, they uncover a darker truth—Nation Builders, Inc. (formerly the Killing Committee) is operating out of the ruins of the former seat of government, the Pyramid, to manipulate global regimes. And they've built their own AI.

Now, Reis must outwit the puppet masters who shattered their home, confront betrayals on every front, and hold on to Edgar—and their dream of a free, reunified Twin City-States of Anver-Kasyova.

KILLING MOTIVES

Killing Games, Book Three

Reis Asher

Chapter One

REIS

Reis hit the ground as a bullet sank into the car door above their head, missing them by inches. Smashing into the concrete knocked the wind out of their lungs, and they gasped. Recovering quickly, they rolled underneath the vehicle, trying to buy themself a few precious seconds to think. Reis's heart pounded. Blood roared in their ears, the din of their body complementing the rain hitting the car like a percussion backing track.

So much for gathering evidence. They'd barely ventured a mile into Anver before being fired upon by an unknown sniper. Careless. Reis could hear Edgar telling them it was a bad idea, but they'd pleaded to go on this scouting mission. After receiving a report that the once grand technological powerhouse of Anver was now home to starvation, pestilence, war, and death on a scale befitting the apocalypse, they were determined to see it with their own eyes.

Anver's people were dying, and Reis felt duty-bound

to help. Sitting in relative safety on the other side of the river in Kasyova wasn't cutting it. A soldier had to take action, not make statements and wish for the best. Fighting was in their blood, trained into them from an early age, and their skills were being tested once again.

Another shot made Reis jerk involuntarily as it shattered a window. Now wasn't the time to indulge in reverie, with crystalline nuggets of safety glass raining down on the pavement like hail, inches away. Eventually, even the most amateur sniper would find their target, if only with a ricochet. Reis wouldn't lie here and wait for the enemy to get lucky.

There was no way they could escape without being fired upon, so negotiation was the only option. Reis hoped they were dealing with a scared citizen instead of a mercenary from one of the many military contracting groups divvying up Anver like a pie.

"I don't want to hurt you!" Reis yelled out into the pouring rain. "There's no need for us to fight. I'm on your side." They closed their eyes, wondering if their voice carried over the sound of the rain. They were done here if they couldn't use reason to talk their way out of danger. Their only hope was that their would-be assassin would run out of bullets, and they could make a run for it.

Reis jumped when a response came loud and clear. The sniper was closer to their position than they'd anticipated.

"I saw you emerge from the tunnel. Quit rubbernecking and go back to Kasyova where you belong!" The deep, husky voice held more than a tinge of sadness beneath its anger, and Reis could tell their adversary had been through more in the past year than they cared to consider. They were desperate. That was something Reis could use.

"I just want to talk. We have yet to learn what's been happening since communications were lost. A flyover can only tell us so much. We need to hear from the people on the ground. People like you," Reis explained. "I want to help. Please."

"It's too late for help. While you sat in your ivory towers, we died. There's nothing left to save."

Reis heard sloshing as footfalls kicked up puddles. Strong arms reached under the car and pulled Reis out. They looked up and saw a middle-aged man with a scruffy beard pointing a rifle at their head. All they could do was stay as still as possible, knowing that any sudden move could set off the stranger's itchy trigger finger.

"Get up," the man barked.

Reis rolled onto their side and used the car to crawl to their feet. They were wet and miserable, but this was the closest they'd gotten to engaging with a non-hostile in months. They reached out with one mucky hand, and the man grasped it with an equally filthy one and shook firmly. A warmth in his eyes seemed to radiate from beneath his war-weary cynicism, and Reis decided to rely on their gut instinct that this man could be trusted.

"I'm Reis. Reis Asher," Reis said. "I'm with the Rainbow Bridge. We're a non-governmental organization focused on helping people trapped here."

"NGO? Hah, figures. Fucking government wouldn't risk breaking a nail for Anverites. I thought Tony Anvas was a sad sack of shit, but he was right about one thing—Kasyova never did give a fuck about us." He wiped the rain from his eyes with a frustrated, nasal grunt. His short black hair had grown out and hung over his eyes. He slicked it back in a motion that said he'd give anything for a decent hairdresser or, failing that, a pair of shears to lop it off himself.

"It's complicated." Reis wanted to defend the Kasyovan government, but they were as frustrated with the current stalemate as the stranger seemed to be. The government appeared to have fallen silent, allowing Anver to decay rather than risk a war with one or several of the factions fighting in the civil war—or, more likely, the nations backing them. The Anverite civil war was nothing more than a proxy war that had become a place for the wealthiest nations to air their grievances to one another without risking their citizens or territory.

"It's not so complicated. Kasyova would have come to our aid if we were still the Twin City-States. They would have rolled the tanks in and stopped Anvas before he could kill the President." The man sighed. "In the end, none of that matters. We're way past politics now. All we can do is hope to survive. We take each day at a time, hoping that the big money will lose interest sooner or later and let a faction win. We don't even care who at this point. Let it be the most fanatical separatist blowhards; I don't give a shit. I want it to be over so we can start to rebuild. I'm Zach Fisher, by the way. I used to be a computer programmer. Now I'm just an idiot who knows a language nobody here speaks. I wish I'd become a doctor—we still need those."

"My fiancé is a programmer," Reis explained. "His name is Ed. We still need your skills—perhaps more than ever. You might not believe it, but we're fighting for you. Maybe not with guns or tanks, but we're fighting. Would you believe it if I told you that Tony Anvas is still alive, sunning it up on a private island? The assassination was a hoax. Without hackers, the world would still be hunting me down for his murder."

"If I hadn't heard your name before, I'd write you off as a conspiracy nut." Zach spat. "But even if you're telling the truth and not spewing some 'truther' bullshit, it's not like it matters. This war isn't about ideology anymore. The sides are all the same. It's about foreign actors settling their grudges while padding their bottom line. I'm sure the world reacted to the coup with horror, right? Of course, they didn't. It's just one more war in a country they've never visited and can't even place on a map."

Reis nodded. Zach wasn't wrong, and it hurt to feel cynicism ring true. "Come back to Kasyova with me. I'm sure there's a lot you can tell us about what's going on here. It's been a while since we've encountered anyone willing to hold their fire long enough to talk."

"It's a little late to launch a rescue mission now. As you said before—it's complicated." Zach looked down at the ground, and Reis got the sense there was something he wasn't telling them.

"Do you have a family? They can come, too, if you'd like. We want to help the people on this side, Zach. Let me help you."

"I can't accept your help." Zach turned on his heel. "A year ago, I could have used you—but now. No. Just go back to your pretty little city on the other side of the river and forget you ever saw me."

"I can't do that," Reis said. "I was born in Anver. Before the crisis, I was a Bureau agent. The citizens of Anver are my responsibility."

"It's been a year since the coup. A whole fucking year of hell on earth. A year of waiting for help that never came. Where have you been? What took you so fucking long to cross a three-mile-wide river with a tunnel underneath?"

Reis lowered their gaze. They'd been recovering. Finding themself. Putting their own oxygen mask on before they could assist the person next to them. It was hard to look at Zach—one of those left behind—and tell him the truth, but if they were to have any chance at success, they had to be completely honest.

"I was—there were some things I had to take care of. Hormones. Surgery. PTSD from the last few times I've been in fear for my life. I wasn't exactly in a condition to scout out a war zone. I shouldn't even be here now. I'd much rather be living in my ivory tower, planning my wedding, but I'm not. I wasn't here for you a year ago, but I'm here now."

"You're trans?" Zach raised one eyebrow. "Heh. Go figure."

"What's that supposed to mean?" Reis asked, raising their defenses. It had been a long time since they'd encountered phobia of any kind, but who knew what had happened to Anverite society since being cut off.

"It means you ain't the only one." Zach kicked a puddle. "Thank fuck most of the effects of T are non-reversible—but not all." He shook his head. "I'm forgetting my manners. It's been so long since I needed 'em. Pronouns?"

"They/them," Reis elaborated. "I'm transmasc."

Zach nodded. "Just masc here, all the way. Fine, I'll come with you—but I need to get something first. Back at my house, right up the hill here." Zach led Reis across a pock-marked street. Weeds pushed through the tarmac, breaking the road where grenades and IEDs hadn't done the job. Reis followed Zach up crumbling steps to a decrepit house that was once a jewel of suburbia. It was only a few miles from where Reis and Edgar had shared a home once upon a time. Reis had often wondered if it still stood and what state it was in now.

"This was your house before the war?" Reis asked.

Zach nodded. "Yeah. My wife and I lived here. Now it's just me."

"I'm sorry," Reis said.

"Don't misunderstand. She isn't dead. She left me for some prick who could offer her the food and protection I couldn't. I should be bitter about it, but she wasn't wrong. I couldn't protect her. Couldn't even protect myself." Zach unlocked the front door and hustled inside. "Now I find out if you're here to help me."

Reis heard it, then. A baby's cry echoed from upstairs. Zach's eyes narrowed, and he stomped upstairs. The child's screams fell silent. Reis kicked off their muddy boots and climbed the creaking stairs, not wanting to soil the dirty carpet any more than it already was. Decrepit or not, this was someone's home. The door to the upstairs bedroom was open, and Zach's binder lay on the bed. He held the baby to his chest, nursing it. Reis looked away, feeling like they were intruding on a private moment.

They hadn't felt dysphoria since their top surgery, but there it was, loud and clear, and judging from Zach's look, he felt it every time he fed the tiny infant in his arms. Reis backed up and waited outside until Zach emerged.

"I can't imagine how hard this has to be for you." Reis blinked back tears, suddenly angry that Zach was forced to be here, birthing and nursing a baby alone against his will.

"You get it. I'll go with you on one condition," Zach said. "You find a good home for her because I can't do this anymore. I need to finish my transition. This should never have happened in the first place. It wasn't supposed to happen, but I couldn't get T after the war started and..." He leaned against the wall, eyes squeezed shut, gathering his composure.

Reis let him be for a moment, swallowing the lump in their throat at the nightmarish scenario. "Of course, we'll help you. Adoption services, transition services, therapy... The Kasyovan government will fund all of it. They've been cutting the Rainbow Bridge checks on the down-low this past year because they do care. They can't show it because their hands are tied by superpowers threatening to invade if they intervene in Anver's 'efforts for independence.'"

Zach sighed. "Whatever. I don't care about politics. Just get me out of this hellhole. Please. Get me to where I need to be, Reis. If you can't take us both, take her. Find her the family she needs."

"You're both coming. Pack the things you need. We need to move out before nightfall."

"What about your contact?" Zach asked.

"They didn't show up at the rendezvous," Reis explained. "I'm going to assume they're dead. Let me know what you need to pack, and we'll get going." They took a deep breath, steadying themself on shaky legs before muttering, "Fuck. How did things get so messed up in just a year?" They grabbed a bag and started packing things Zach laid out on the bed. Most of it was for the baby—Zach had done an incredible job, given his impossible situation. The child slept soundly, oblivious to the fact that she was going on a journey very soon.

"Reis, come in."

Reis started as their two-way radio came to life. They'd agreed to use the frequency sparingly since there was no way to keep the channel private from listening ears.

"Go ahead," Reis replied.

"Are you on your way? It's getting dark outside." Edgar's voice was heavily tinged with concern, and it was comforting. Reis wanted nothing more than to be back in his arms. They smiled wanly, realizing transition had changed everything. Once, it had been easy to put their life on the line. Now, with so much to return home to, it was hard to walk through the fire and pretend it didn't affect them.

"Everything's fine," Reis said, not wanting to go into too much detail. "I met someone, but not the contact. I'll be coming back with company this time."

A tiny sigh carried over the frequency. "Reis…are you sure that's wise?"

"Yes. Trust me on this. You'll understand when you meet him. Heading back to the rendezvous in five. Reis out."

"He sounds reluctant." Zach paused his packing for a moment. "You're not supposed to bring people back, are you?"

"It wasn't the goal of this mission, no, but we do help people escape Anver. There haven't been many non-hostile survivors lately. I think Edgar's just surprised and probably a little paranoid. Hackers, you know?"

Zach laughed. "Yeah, you're not wrong. When you know how computers work, you understand their flaws and know they can't be trusted to keep you secure. When you see inside information that confirms a conspiracy, it tells you the same thing about people."

"Right." Reis nodded. "Ed was right—we should move soon. I like the cover of darkness in some ways, but I know it's unsafe after dark." They slung a backpack over their shoulders and carried a separate shoulder bag, leaving their gun hand free in case they needed to draw their pistol quickly. Zach picked up the baby with care and held her close to him.

"What's her name?" Reis asked.

"I didn't—I haven't named her," Zach admitted. "That probably sounds callous, doesn't it?"

Zach didn't wait for a response. He pushed past Reis into the hallway and padded down the stairs with the child in his arms. Reis followed, trying to find words that felt right as they settled into a manageable pace that could accommodate their load.

Reis shrugged. They were indifferent to children and sensed Zach felt the same way. "It's not insensitive at all. What's in a child's name, anyway? If you're not keeping her, it makes no sense to give her a name."

Zach nodded but said nothing. The rain had mostly abated, but the air was thick and heavy with moisture, making it feel like they were breathing liquid. The sun had disappeared below the horizon, giving way to darkness.

Zach said little on their long walk. Reis made a couple of aborted attempts at conversation before deciding it was a wasted effort. The noise only compromised their attempts at staying off the radar. The city was eerily quiet—too quiet, in Reis's opinion. The hair on the back of their neck stood on end as they ventured through the rubble of houses and streets Reis used to know like the back of their hand. It looked nothing like the Anver they remembered, disfigured and divided by the city's various factions.

"The tunnel's in this house," Reis said, leading Zach into the derelict building. After the old tunnel entrance had been destroyed, they'd had to dig the tunnel in a different direction and choose a new neighborhood to house the exit. It had taken months of precious time, and they'd been sure they'd been discovered on multiple occasions. It was bold to reuse the tunnel after its dramatic compromise and collapse, but sometimes, hiding in plain sight was the best option. It was better than trying to make the river crossing, a sitting duck in a boat for the three-mile crossing. "How did you know about it, anyway?"

"Rumor. Word on the street is that help comes from this way via a tunnel under the river, but nobody has ever seen it first-hand, so I thought it was hearsay. Go figure, though—there it is." Zach peered into the tunnel as Reis lifted the metal trapdoor in the abandoned house's basement. Reis ushered for Zach to go first. They didn't feel safe until they pulled the metal door down over the entrance again. Only then did they allow themselves a sigh of relief.

"Hard part's done," Reis said. "Now we walk for three miles. We'll emerge in Kasyova. A car will be waiting for us." They adjusted the heavy shoulder bag and took the lead. The immediate danger had passed, but the dysphoria triggered by what they'd seen lingered like a dark shadow on a sunny day. They saw themself if they'd stayed in Anver, trapped on an island that had returned to savagery. It was a grim reminder that the veneer of civilization could be stripped away from even the most advanced nations, given the right conditions.

Reis could easily be Zach, pregnant and forced to endure a body that betrayed them more and more each day, and they shuddered, knowing how close they'd come to staying in Anver out of guilt. If it hadn't been for Edgar reminding them they deserved a shot at happiness, no matter what was happening in the world...

No. There was no use dwelling on it. Reis cut off their dark thoughts and continued through the tunnel, concentrating on the pain of the heavy shoulder bag strap digging into their shoulder to ground themself. That they could endure.

In Zach's position, they doubted they could have been as brave as he was, and they didn't pause to think about the other options. It wasn't worth considering the path not traveled. They had to focus on what came next.

Chapter Two

EDGAR

Edgar watched the red blip exit the tunnel on his map of Anver-Kasyova and released the long breath he'd been holding. He and Reis had faced death together so many times, yet it seemed to get harder to bear, not easier, as time passed. Their roots had become entangled, and now he wasn't sure he could live without his partner. He wondered how he felt about that, but perhaps it had been true from the moment they'd met. As independent and successful as he'd been on his own, Edgar had been no match for the Killing Committee. Without Reis, he wouldn't be alive. It pained him to think that Reis didn't rely on him as much as he relied on them.

"Packages are safe and secure, Ed," Teon said over the radio in their rich, velveteen voice. Their voice sounded heavier than usual; tinged with feeling, as though they were on the edge of tears, and Edgar had to hold himself back from asking if Reis was all right. Of course, Reis was all right—Teon had said "safe and secure," not "damaged in transit" or "compromised." That didn't stop Edgar from cutting into the Kasyovan closed-circuit camera system, following the vehicle back to their office, kicking his chair away from the desk, and practically running to the front door when it pulled up outside. He felt a little pathetic waiting in the doorway like a puppy anticipating the return of its master. He sighed as Reis emerged from the vehicle, the tension that had kept him awake so late into the night ebbing away and leaving a sense of exhaustion heavy in his veins.

When the passenger side door opened, and a man holding a baby alighted, Edgar knew he would need another cup of coffee. Reis always seemed to bring trouble with them. They were such a sap for hopeless causes, but Edgar could hardly fault them for that, even if the government money was running dry. Still, Edgar had never known them to get excited over babies. He'd tested the waters to find Reis's opinions were similar to his own—babies were needy, loud, and often disgusting—and even asking the question had seemed to trigger a hefty amount of dysphoria in Reis to the point he'd never asked about it again. He hadn't needed to. He was quite happy with the life he'd built with Reis and their friends, especially since they'd fled to Kasyova. They didn't need anything else to be a family.

But of course, Reis still protected the vulnerable, personal needs be damned. That was what made them special.

Reis briefly embraced Edgar, then turned to the man next to him. "This is Zach," Reis said. "His daughter doesn't have a name yet, but we need to get Zach set up with adoption, medical, and transition resources ASAP."

"Trans—oh." Edgar put the pieces together before he could put his foot in his mouth and was grateful for Reis's heads-up.

"Nice to meet you, Zach." Edgar held out his hand, and Zach took it. He shook firmly with the hand not cradling the baby to his chest. Teon flapped about in the background like a hen, and Edgar was glad to let them take control. Teon ushered Zach into a side room where the Rainbow Bridge emergency nurse kept her office and shut the door behind them.

"You okay?" Edgar asked as casually as he could manage. He could see the strain on Reis's face, the exhaustion in their bloodshot eyes, and the general slump in their stance.

"You broke protocol by calling me on the mission," Reis chided him. "You can see my location on GPS."

"I'm sorry. Something about this trip had my hackles up in the first place. I'm glad you could help someone, but I'm not going to say I'm not worried about our contact being a no-show."

"Things are bad over there," Reis said. "Way worse than the drone images show. It's so quiet. Like the city's waiting for something. Or there's just nobody left."

Edgar nodded. "Yeah, the last few drones I flew over gave me the same impression. Perhaps the war is finally winding down, Reis. This could be good for us."

"You're just hoping the war ends before the money runs out," Reis observed. "How much do we have left?"

"A few thousand. Probably enough to help Zach out before we're on our own." Edgar sighed. "I've tried crowdfunding, but let's face it: the people of Kasyova think Anver brought this war on themselves. They're not as compassionate and considerate as I would have hoped."

"What about that other thing you've been looking into?" Reis stared into Edgar's eyes, their pupils large and pleading in the low light. It wasn't easy for either of them to consider the end of the road. Everything they'd built was slowly crumbling into the river, eroded by time and a lack of funds. Kasyova seemed content to let Anver fall apart, and it seemed there was no path back to the way things had been before.

Edgar sighed, ushering Reis into his office and closing the door. He didn't want Teon to hear about his backup plan. They wouldn't like it one bit. "It's feasible but a last resort and not without risk. If the Kasyovan government finds out I plan to install a botnet on their network to mine cryptocurrency, I'll be doing some serious time."

"It's not like you're stealing money, and it's their security flaw," Reis argued. "Fuck them. They could offer more help but are too worried about what the Union States will think."

"With good reason. The Union States could crush us in an instant." Edgar bit his lip.

"They'd never do it. Public opinion is against it. Forcing military action on a country for defending its natural ally would destroy the President," Reis argued.

"Not like they'd need to roll the tanks in. Kasyova can't afford sanctions."

Reis sighed and sat down in a plastic chair. Edgar returned to his network of computers, their monitors providing the only light in the dark room. Fans whirring filled the silence for a few moments as they sat at their usual impasse. There was no easy answer to the war or their funding problems. Even if all sides forged a truce and international governments got bored of their proxy war, the looming humanitarian crisis would take more than a little Kasyovan intervention to fix.

"Zach hit a nerve, didn't he?" Edgar asked, breaking the silence.

"Yeah. For months, I thought that perhaps it wouldn't be such a terrible thing if the Rainbow Bridge folded. I couldn't help but think we'd done everything we could. But when I saw Zach's desperate situation, I was angry at myself for turning my back on the people of Anver when they needed us the most. That, and...Zach could have been me if things had rolled out a little differently. I can't even stand the thought of what he went through. The body dysphoria of carrying a child to term and feeding her must have been awful..."

Edgar nodded. Reis didn't need to say anymore. He clutched his hands together underneath the desk, fighting the urge to go around the desk and pull Reis close to him. His comfort wasn't the priority right now, and he stifled his own need to give Reis some space to sort through their feelings.

"The Twin City-States weren't perfect, but they were

utopia compared to what Anver's going through now. I wish I could turn back time and change everything. I feel so powerless." Reis buried their head in their hands, forcing calm, measured breaths through their nose.

"We couldn't have stopped Anvas's plot. Better people than us tried, remember?" Edgar's mind strayed to Emily Vos, killed at her wedding by a spy loyal to Anvas, of the Bureau agents gunned down in Anvas's gutting of law enforcement. The military minds twisted and turned to support Anvas's coup against the government. The President and his cabinet shuffled off the mortal coil like puppets being discarded after the show.

A loud knock sounded at the front door, rattling the screen door so hard that Edgar heard it shake on its hinges. He stood up, glad the darkness and the ethereal glow of the monitors covered his paling face. Nighttime visits were never good news.

"Bureau agents! Open up!"

Edgar paused in his tracks as he stood in the vestibule. What the hell could Kasyovan Bureau agents want with them? Figuring any delay in his response could be risky, he steeled himself for trouble and opened the door. Three Bureau agents pushed past Edgar without a word. They entered the nurse's office and pulled Zach out abruptly. Zach looked at Reis with confusion and despair.

Reis stood in the doorway to Edgar's office. "Let go of him immediately! What do you think you're doing?"

"Take in our Anverite Bureau friend there," the ranking agent said. "The hacker, too. Leave the baby and the others. We'll come back if need be." Edgar shot Reis a horrified glance as he was cuffed. This had to be some misunderstanding. They'd clear this up at the Bureau office, and everything would return to normal.

Edgar went without a struggle. Reis followed behind, resentment and betrayal shining in their eyes when Edgar looked back at them. He and Reis were bundled into a black Bureau-issue car while Zach was thrust into the one behind. The vehicle took off at speed, jerking Edgar around in his seat as a million thoughts raced through his mind. Had the Kasyovan government been spying on their activities and determined they'd done something illegal? Was it the cryptocurrency plan? Why would Zach be involved?

Edgar's eyes met Reis's, asking the silent question: what did we do wrong? Reis shrugged. They had no answer, but Edgar had a bad feeling in the pit of his stomach.

Something was badly wrong—and they were about to find out what.

Chapter Three

REIS

"I want to see my lawyer." Reis's first words were calm and measured when they sat in the cold, stark interrogation room. They weren't going to show the agents they were rattled. They would turn the agents' tricks back on them and agitate them into spilling their secrets.

"You don't need a lawyer." The lead agent who had arrested them paced the room. He was short in stature, with small, dark, almond-shaped eyes, tawny skin, and black hair tied in a small ponytail. His blank stare and stoic expression gave nothing away, but Reis noted his stance. He was tense, guarded—afraid, even. Afraid of what?

"I'm being detained against my will, and not one of you has given me a clear reason," Reis pressed.

The lead agent gave them a sharp look. "Relax. We're on the same side here."

The door opened, and another agent held two cups of coffee. Reis couldn't determine their gender from one glance, but they were tall and pale, with piercing, narrow blue eyes and black hair shaped in a pixie cut. To Reis's surprise, the agent placed the second cup of coffee in front of them and unlocked their handcuffs.

"If you're trying to play good cop, go elsewhere," Reis said. "I know your tricks. I was a Bureau agent myself. I've had the same training as you."

"Then you know it's not standard to give a detainee a scalding hot beverage which could be used as a weapon," the ranking agent said. "Or to unlock their handcuffs." He leaned against the wall, his eyes straying to the door.

"I want to know why I'm here," Reis insisted. "You have my fiancé and a friend of ours, too. I demand their immediate release."

"That would not be a good idea right now," the lead agent said. "I suggest you make yourself comfortable, Mx. Asher. My name is Special Agent Hikaru Wynn, and this is my subordinate, Agent Rain Odell. We're with the Kasyovan Bureau."

"Funny, I don't remember Kasyova giving a damn. Why are you interested in me now?" Reis bit their tongue. They'd meant to stay calm, but Wynn had hit a sore spot. The Kasyovan government's deafening silence at the human tragedy unfolding in Anver was stuck beneath their skin like a splinter they couldn't get out.

"They're oblivious," Odell said. "Looks like you'll have to explain everything from the beginning, sir."

"Apparently. Reis—can I call you Reis?—think carefully. Think about the situation Kasyova is in. Could we afford to tie an asset as valuable as you and your team up in red tape and government bureaucracy?"

"What are you talking about?" Reis asked.

"On its surface, Kasyova appears indifferent to Anver's suffering. You've expressed frustration at it yourself, haven't you?" Wynn said. "It's only gotten worse with time. All official support of your Rainbow Bridge organization ceased last month without explanation. Haven't you wondered why?"

Reis shook their head. "I know why. The Union States have threatened sanctions if Kasyova interferes with the civil war in Anver. That apparently extends to us now, too—even though we're an NGO on the books."

"Even private payments can be tracked. Tony Anvas and the organization he works for—Nation Builders Inc.—have some of the world's best intelligence assets and hackers at their disposal. Kasyova allowed those payments to go through only because they wanted them to be seen." Wynn shrugged. "Nation Builders knew the Kasyovan government would make an effort to change the situation. It would be suspicious if they didn't. Your organization provided a good smokescreen, but time is running out, and we need you on the inside."

"The inside?" Reis's eyes widened. "What do you mean?"

"What I'm about to tell you is highly classified information. One word of it outside this building, and you will find yourself imprisoned at a black site at Kasyova's pleasure. If you'd rather not know, Reis, I suggest you tell me now, and we'll let you and your friends go back to your little lives playing the good guys. I promise you;

you'd rather be in the know."

Reis paused. They knew this information would put them at risk and pull them back into the world of conspiracy they'd fled, yet the thought of flailing about in the dark trying to save people like Zach one at a time seemed like a futile effort. If there was some way to draw upon more resources, if there was more going on beneath the surface, the only logical thing to do was to take the risk and step inside.

Reis hoped Edgar would forgive them. "I'm in."

"Let's go for a walk." Wynn ushered them over. Reis stood up, bringing the coffee cup with them. The coffee was warm, creamy, and sweet, just as they liked. They followed Wynn and Odell out of the interrogation room and down a hallway without windows. Harsh fluorescent lights cast a flickering glare over the hallway. Reis walked past Edgar's cell and lingered a moment. Agents stood with him, and the look on his face was one of confusion and shock.

"He can't see you—that's a one-way window. He will have his own choice to make, Reis. You must honor that, even if it means keeping absolute silence about what you learn here to the person you love most," Wynn said.

Wynn and Odell kept walking. Reis sped up to keep pace with them. They reached the end of the corridor, and Odell pressed a button to call an elevator. Reis waited in silence. Had they made the right choice? Only time would tell.

The elevator arrived, and the doors slid open. Reis stepped inside after the agents. Odell pressed the button for B10. The doors closed with a final thud that made them wonder if they were ever coming back.

"Level B10? We're going underground?" Reis asked.

"That is correct," Wynn said. "These walls are shielded by three-inch thick lead and steel, and a dampening field stops cellphone communication, Wi-Fi signals, and deep scanning. It was originally designed as a fallout shelter for the government in case of nuclear war, but we have more important threats to deal with than radiation." The elevator stopped, and the doors opened onto a great hall modeled after the Anver-Kasyova Senate. It was a hive of activity, with people milling about, seemingly oblivious to the intruders in their midst.

"Welcome," Wynn said, "to the Twin City-States Shadow Government."

"What?" Reis's eyes widened. "I don't understand."

"Think about it. The Union States and their threats tie Kasyova's hands. Not to mention Nation Builders, who infiltrated every agency in the Twin City-States before the coup. We were late, and Anvas was able to destroy Anver's government—but not completely. The President and many others in the Senate were killed, but others survived, and we brought them inside. Same with the Bureau and the military. As Anvas purged, we recruited. People who proved their loyalty and worth to the Twin City-States slowly formed this new government underground. The puppets upstairs in the Kasyovan Senate keep up a good show of maintaining neutrality and keeping the country running, but we hold the real power."

"If that's true, why haven't you done more to save

Anver? There's nothing left but a shell of the old city!"

"We've done all we can," Odell explained. "Even working independently of rules, treaties, and regulations, we can't afford to be too obvious and blow our cover. This government is a clandestine operation."

"Why did you bring me in on this, and why now?" Reis asked.

"We'll get to that," Wynn said. "First, there's someone I'd like you to meet. Back in the elevator, if you would."

Reis stepped back into the elevator and watched the doors slide shut, questions swirling through their mind. They quelled their rage, trying to piece together the shadow government's place in all this. Was the quiet in Anver their doing? Were they bringing Reis in because they had a plan to end the war once and for all? What had they been doing down here for a year?

The doors opened again on a bare, white hallway with tiles that squeaked underfoot and an astringent smell. Reis looked around, dazed by the bright lights and confused by their presence.

People who proved their loyalty and worth to the Twin City-States slowly formed this new government underground.

"That can't be possible," Reis whispered. They ran to the door Wynn held open and entered a tiny hospital room. The woman's face looked familiar, but there were so many tubes and wires hooked up that it took Reis a moment to recognize Emily Vos. "That's not possible. Emily died!"

"That's what Anvas thought, too. So much so that he didn't bother to send his agents to the hospital to check. We rescued her, but she hasn't woken from her coma—and doctors warn that even if she does, she won't be the same person. She's suffered brain damage, and we won't know the extent of it until she wakes."

Reis reached beneath the sheet and took Emily's hand in their own. It was pale and thin, so unlike the Emily they knew it was hard to recognize this body as hers.

Reis realized they were crying, tears forming silent rivers on their face as hope and despair collided. Emily was alive...sort of. Trapped between life and death, yet, as horrific as her injuries were, it was a miracle to see her chest rise and fall, to look at her face and think those eyes might one day see again. It was a miracle. Emily was alive. Anver-Kasyova was alive. Reis closed their eyes and balled their free hand into a fist, fighting the urge to abandon all dignity and sob uncontrollably in front of Odell and Wynn.

"She was the one who made all this possible, Reis," Wynn explained. "She got close to one of Anvas's deep cover agents. Richard Emmaus was so in love with her that he spilled part of the coup plot. She transmitted that data to other loyalists. She saved many lives. Realizing his mistake, Emmaus tried one last-ditch effort to silence her by blowing himself up at the wedding, as you know."

"I can't believe she did all this and never said anything. I would have helped her. Didn't you trust me, Emily?"

"On the contrary—she listed you as her most trust-worthy agent. That's why we've let you operate independently for so long. You've gathered valuable intel for us and covered our operations here. We're only bringing you in because we're ready to move on Anver, Tony Anvas, and Nation Builders. We'd like you to be involved in taking Anver back and reuniting our nation once again."

Reis shot them a glance. They were in if the plan was to put a gun in their hand, but they had the sense it extended much deeper than that. "Be involved? How?"

"The Shadow Government has everything we need—except a President. When the last President was killed, we pledged to hold free and fair elections once Anver was free again, but this war has continued longer than we would have liked. The people are bitter and broken. They won't let Anver fall back into being a part of the Twin City-States again, especially when they believe that Kasyova has done nothing for them all this time. That's why we need you: Reis Asher, child of Elias Torrell, the father of Unification. Your name still holds weight and commands respect in Anver. We're ready to swoop in and win the war as soon as we remove Nation Builders, Inc. A recent election in the Union States has meant they care less about this proxy war with the Eastern Federation than they did. If we take Anver back, they won't strike against us."

"How do you plan to take down Anvas and Nation Builders?" Reis asked.

"That's on a need-to-know basis," Wynn explained. "If you decide to become our interim President, you'll have access to everything. You'll get to call the shots."

"I have to think about this," Reis said. "President? I'm—I'm a soldier, not a politician!"

"On the contrary. Your service and dedication to the Twin City-States have proven absolute loyalty on your part. You've had the best interests of others at heart since the Killing Game incident four years ago. You're the best person for the job, Reis. Of course, if you want to wait for your fiancé to decide and consult with him if possible, that's understandable. The final operation to unseat Nation Builders isn't underway yet, so we'll happily take you to a room and let you rest."

"Please," Reis said. Their head spun. President? They had to be dreaming. Or perhaps it was a nightmare. Were they equipped to lead?

"Odell, see that Reis gets settled comfortably." Wynn reached out his hand and took Reis's, shaking it again. "Regardless of your decision, I'm honored to have met you, Reis. Thank you for your service to your country." Wynn let Reis's hand slip from his grasp, turned on his heel, and started to walk away.

"Wait!" Reis yelled down the hallway. Their voice echoed in the stark, unfurnished corridor. "I have one more question. What does Zach have to do with any of this? Is he one of your agents? Was that situation in Anver a test of my loyalty and stability?"

"Yes, but not in the way you think. The situation was every bit real. Zach worked for the Bureau at the same time you did, in the Data Intelligence Unit. We lost contact with him after the coup and subsequent Bureau massacre. He figured out how to make contact recently, and we discovered that he'd been captured and assaulted by the Rebels. From there—yes, we used you to pick him up. Your mission only convinced the last few doubters that you were the one we wanted to ask to be our leader."

Reis bowed their head. "What's going to happen to him?"

"He'll be offered therapy, of course. His daughter will be offered for adoption if that's what he wishes. We'll extend all the healthcare benefits he would have received as a Bureau employee."

Reis sighed. "That's not my question. Why did you bring him in? He doesn't need to be involved in this."

"Zach has important intel on life in Anver. We're going to need his testimony if we're to rebuild Anver. Drones, flyovers, and spies can only tell us so much about what happened in the past year. I appreciate your desire to protect him after everything he's been through, but ultimately, it's his decision whether he wants to participate in the operation or not."

"Understood." The fight slipped out of Reis, and they let Wynn walk away this time, falling in step behind Odell as they led them back to the elevator.

"Tell me a little bit about yourself," Reis said as the elevator rose to level B6. "I feel like I'm at a loss."

"I'm agender, if you were wondering," Odell said. They pointed to a pronoun pin with they/them pronouns. "I'm a rare one here—I worked for the Kasyovan police when the war started. I chanced upon the Shadow Government by accident while investigating a murder case and finding out the victim was still alive. By then, I had little choice but to throw my hat in the ring. I knew too much. Staying on the outside would have risked both my life and the existence of the Shadow Government. I want nothing more than for the Twin City-States to be reunited, Reis. I hope you're the one who leads the Anver people home to us."

The elevator stopped, and the doors opened. Reis followed automatically as Odell walked down a nondescript hallway and handed Reis a keycard. "This is your room. If your fiancé should come inside, we'll send him here. For now, I would advise you to rest and think about what you want to do. Time is limited, Reis Asher."

Chapter Four

EDGAR

Edgar stood at the entrance to the Shadow Senate with a grin plastered across his face. "Neat. I want to say I already knew, but I'm glad to report that nothing I found in Nation Builders' files even hinted at the possibility of a conspiracy like this. You did your job well."

Wynn's dark, glossy eyes seemed to shine with something Edgar thought was pride, but the man was hard to read. "I would hope for once they are not one step ahead of us, Mr. Tobias. Anyway, I hate to cut our tour short, but I suspect Reis has news of their own to share."

"So, Reis opted to go inside?" Edgar laughed, raising a hand to stop Wynn, who'd opened his mouth to protest. "Of course they did. Never mind." The world seemed a little lighter in the wake of Wynn's revelation. Kasyova did care about Anver. The Twin City-States hadn't died an early death when Tony Anvas shot the President. Here, beneath his home city, hope was alive and well, and the Twin City-States were about to rise from the ashes like a phoenix. "I suppose what I wanted to ask was… Why do you need me? I get why you picked Reis, but I'm a nobody. If you chose me to come inside because I'm Reis's future husband, I'm fine with that, but I'd like to know."

"On the contrary, Mr. Tobias, your hacking skills are on par with our best and brightest. You'll fit right in with our Data Intelligence Unit, who can show you a few new things they've snuck out of Nation Builders' digital vault."

Edgar rested his hands on his hips. "Wow, you managed to hack 128-bit encryption? That's impressive."

"Of course. Along with well-trained agents and a diverse software and malware library, we also have something else you do not: computing power. Our central computer is one of the first general computing artificial intelligences in the world, built by proud Anverites here in Kasyova. We originally planned to install it in the basement of the Glass Pyramid. After the war broke out, we finished our work in the lowest levels of the bunker. 'Oracle,' as we call her, now controls the entire building. Nothing gets in or out without her knowledge, and she has a peak computing power of over five hundred petaflops."

"Wow." Edgar shook his head. "To think I was cracking security on a shitty stock laptop a few months ago. I can't wait to see the brute force attacks Oracle can pull off."

"You sound excited, Mr. Tobias." A feminine voice echoed from a speaker in the hallway, and the air in front of Edgar shimmered until a blue holographic figure of a woman in a long dress appeared in front of him.

"You're Oracle?" Edgar asked.

"Indeed. I like to greet all my Data Intelligence analysts personally. But enough with the introductions. You want to see Reis Asher, am I right?"

Edgar nodded. "Yeah. I can't get my head around this. I need to sit down for a moment. To think I almost chickened out."

"That's not true. I was monitoring your heart rate in the interrogation room. You had no intention of refusing our offer," Oracle said.

"You got me there. I can't turn down a mystery box. I'm the kind of person who would always wonder what was inside."

Wynn broke into the conversation, clearing his throat. "I see you've made your acquaintance with Oracle. I have other things to attend to, so I'll let Oracle show you to your room." He began to walk away, then paused momentarily and turned on his heel to face Edgar. "I assume I don't need to tell you that Oracle is not to be used for mining cryptocurrency, in case you had any such ideas. She's fully self-aware and believe me, she will kick you to the curb and erase your clearances if you try to get inside her head."

"Hey, Agent Wynn, I'm not planning to send our lady down into the mines. My crypto scheme was a desperate measure because I thought Anver's last hope was going broke. I don't need that plan anymore. Though it bothers me that we were so easily compromised."

"It's for the best," Wynn said. "We wanted Nation Builders to see what you were up to. I apologize for the deception, but Rainbow Bridge served as a valuable smokescreen for our efforts here. Tony Anvas believes Kasyova is about to pull all its assets out of Anver for good—which is exactly what we need him to believe."

"He's coming back, isn't he? Now that Anver is nothing but dust, Anvas wants to rebuild it in his image. Am I right?"

"Perceptive," Oracle interjected, her holo-image "leaning" against a wall without clipping into it. "You're almost right. Anvas wants to rebuild Anver as his model city for the rich and powerful—like Dubai, but with fewer foreign princes to bribe for planning rights. He'll hail it as a rebirth of the city, but it really means that ethnic Anverites will be forced into squalid housing while he builds golf courses to entertain foreign dignitaries on affordable land. Anver will become a playground for the wealthy, and its people will be displaced or forced to work in the hospitality industry. Its identity as an emerging technology and science incubator will be lost."

"It's funny. I always pegged Anvas to be some twisted idealist, but it's all about the money for him." Edgar shook his head. "To think he destroyed an entire city just to build his oasis... It makes me sick."

"Would it be better if he was a bitter ideologue spewing ethnic hatred? His motives are irrelevant, Mr. Tobias. Tony Anvas is the sworn enemy of the Twin City-States of Anver-Kasyova. He is a traitor, and we will unseat him and return the Twin Cities to their former glory."

"Right." Edgar grinned like a kid being handed a large piece of chocolate. He hummed one of the Soulmates' songs as Oracle led him down the hallway to an elevator. Wynn broke off and took a different direction. Edgar had more questions than he could count, but he wasn't sure his brain could handle the answers without sleep.

"Is Reis waiting for me?" Edgar asked.

"They are pacing your shared quarters and imbibing a mug of hot chocolate. Judging from their elevated heart rate and tense posture, I must speculate that they are pondering a life-altering decision," Oracle explained.

"There have been a lot of those today," Edgar said. "I can relate." He stopped at a nondescript door as Oracle gestured to it. "This is our room?"

"Indeed. Sleep well, Edgar Tobias. If you have questions, call my name. I am happy to assist you or Reis at any time of the day or night." Oracle disappeared into the wall, disintegrating as she "touched" the surface. Edgar stood with his heart in his mouth, wondering what news Reis could have that was more compelling than what he'd already learned. He knocked on the door, and it slid open at once.

Reis looked up with a mixture of joy and fear in their expression. Edgar hurried over to them and Reis melted in his arms. The door slid shut, leaving them alone in the grand suite they'd been provided. A living room was stocked with furniture so lavish it seemed almost absurd, with gold leaf trim on every accent, while through the door of an adjoining bedroom, Edgar spied the biggest four-poster bed he'd ever laid eyes on. The wallpaper was burgundy with gold trim, and for a moment, Edgar was convinced that he'd stepped into the President's Suite at the Mavarique.

"What is going on?" Edgar said, breaking into a smile. "It's like they've rolled out the red carpet for us."

"They have," Reis said, gazing into Edgar's eyes. "They didn't tell you? They've asked me to be Interim President of the Twin City-States of Anver-Kasyova."

"What?" Edgar's jaw felt slack, and he realized his mouth had fallen open. He opened and closed it several times, forming words with no sound as he tried to figure out what to say. President Reis Asher? Weren't they too young for that kind of responsibility?

"That's not all," Reis said. "Emily Vos is alive. In a coma but alive. I can't... I can't process any of this. I feel like I'm dreaming. I've lived on such a thin strand of hope for so long that I can't cope with a bounty like this. Tell me it's real."

"As far as I know, it's real," Edgar said. "I just had a conversation with a state-of-the-art AI. I had no idea such technology existed in the world, let alone here beneath Kasyova. This was not what I expected when Bureau agents raided our office."

"I don't know what to think. What if it's a trap? What if Anvas is controlling all this somehow? I want to be excited about this place, but it all seems too good to be true, Edgar. I saw Emily die. I held her broken body in my arms and confirmed she had no pulse. But she's down in the hospital ward with her nails painted the same as they were on the day of her wedding. They told me she's the reason any of this was possible..." Reis perched themselves on the edge of a couch, looking like they were ready to collapse from exhaustion. "I can't even wrap my head around becoming President. Why me? I'm just a lost soul who stumbled into a conspiracy. I never thought something like this could happen. I don't want that kind of responsibility."

"That's why you're the right person to be the Twin City-States' leader right now. Think about it, Reis. So many power-hungry factions have torn Anver apart with their greed and possessiveness. Tony Anvas wants to dominate and destroy. By shouldering a duty instead of lusting after money, you will give Anver what it's needed since the President was shot—a public servant."

Reis threw their hands up, and Edgar realized he'd said the wrong thing, piling on the pressure when Reis was already set to blow. "I'm not qualified. I'm no politician! I'm too young for this!"

"I don't think they need you to be, Reis. You're not here to rule. Anver needs a figurehead, someone to be a bastion of light after the year of darkness its citizens have endured. They need a hero to remind them why they welcomed Unification in the first place. What better choice than the child of the man who invented the idea? What better choice than someone who put their own life on the line for a stranger, someone who fought for their country against all odds? You can step down and call elections when the Twin City-States are reunited. Until then, I think you're the best choice. Perhaps the only choice."

"I can't make a decision right now," Reis said, tugging at their hair. "We both need sleep. I'm exhausted after the mission. I need to rest and let this all sink in before making any hasty decisions." They wandered into the bedroom, and Edgar followed, his euphoria giving way to pure enervation. The bed looked like a cloud, and Edgar stripped off his clothes and climbed underneath the covers with all the grace he would at home.

With Reis nestled beside him, he slept.

Chapter Five

REIS

Reis jerked awake. The malevolent afterimage of a night-mare grew faint, leaving only a sense of gloom and a bad taste in Reis's mouth. Reis reached for Edgar and found only empty space. Edgar was still an early riser.

Reis got out of bed and padded to the bathroom, where they relieved themselves with a tiny sigh. They stood up, flushed the toilet, and walked over to look in the mirror. The changes Reis's low dose testosterone brought left them feeling more like themself every time they had a chance to gaze at their reflection. It was like coming home.

Eventually, though, they would stop taking it. Not yet, but long before their hair succumbed to male-pattern baldness. The stubble on their chin was pleasant to touch, but they shaved it before it could become anything close to a beard. There were still aspects of femininity they wanted to keep that defined them as a nonbinary person living outside the typical norms of male and female.

For now, though, they were comfortable in their skin in a way they'd never been. It was strange to see their body as an ally instead of an enemy; to watch features they'd only imagined in moments of painful longing finally exist in reality. There was a ghost in the mirror, too—Reis's father, looking back at them a little more each day.

Reis glanced away. Their father had held all the cards as Reis did now. He'd clutched the reins of power in his hands and brought Unification into being, only to betray that ideal down the line. Could Reis be trusted with the Presidency? Could they hold the Twin City-States in the palm of their hand and avoid making the same mistakes their father had?

A polite knock on the bathroom door made Reis start. They walked to the door and opened it to see Edgar standing with a tray full of breakfast balanced in one hand.

"I didn't think you'd be up already. I was hoping to surprise you with breakfast." Edgar walked over to the bedside table and set the tray down.

Reis smiled and climbed back into bed. "I suppose I can be convinced to stay in bed a little longer. If I become President, I don't suppose I'll get a good night's sleep for months."

"You sound like you've made up your mind," Edgar said, grabbing his tray and clambering back into bed beside Reis.

"Wynn sounded like he needed an answer sooner rather than later. From what he told me, the operation to unseat Nation Builders is ready to go and is just waiting on an authority figure to give it the green light. I don't have time to mull over my doubts. This is the role they brought me in to play, and I have no real objections, so why not? If it helps the Twin City-States, I'll do whatever it takes."

"What if you're just being used?" Edgar asked.

"Oh, I'm being used. I'm just not sure that matters," Reis argued. "The Shadow Government needs a figure-head, and they've chosen me to lead. I'm sure they have hidden motives, but why would I decline if their goal is Reunification and the end of Nation Builders' interference?"

Edgar nodded but remained silent for a moment before finally speaking. "After this, we'll get ready and let the Shadow Senate know you've decided. The sooner we can strike Nation Builders, the better for us."

Reis looked into Edgar's eyes, fearing the clarity and intelligence they saw there. Edgar was right; they could feel it in their bones. "You're afraid Tony Anvas is on to the Shadow Government?"

"He's been ahead of us so far. With the number of people down here, it's not inconceivable that one or more of them could be spies. I'm sure Wynn knows that time is running out."

"Delaying my decision won't help matters, no matter how afraid I am that I'm not ready for this." Reis shoveled egg into their mouth like eating was a chore, suddenly less hungry than before. They considered how easily they'd been manipulated...brought in without a choice, given the impossible decision of whether to be involved in Anver's destiny, followed by the one-two punch of Emily's survival and the hope that the Twin City-States might not be lost after all. Everything had been designed to usher Reis into the Presidency without resistance. Reis had no logical reason to rebel against their role, yet the ease with which they accepted it unsettled them.

Something about the big picture still wasn't clear, yet Reis had no choice but to grope forward blindly in the dark, hoping things would turn out all right. They half-heartedly finished their breakfast and stumbled back into the bathroom. They returned to find a pressed suit had been delivered, tailored to their exact measurements. Reis put it on while Edgar showered, then tied the blue tie with the crest of Anver-Kasyova embroidered onto it.

Edgar emerged from the bathroom wrapped in a towel and smirked as he eyed Reis up and down. "You could stand toe-to-toe with any world leader, Reis."

"I didn't even say 'yes' yet, and they made this suit to my precise measurements. I feel like the decision was made for me."

Edgar nodded. "Oracle probably took your measurements as you slept. It might seem creepy, but don't read too much into it. You're not having second thoughts, are you?"

"No."

"Well, then. Enough conspiracy theories. We can't hope to win if we don't trust one another. I know the Shadow Government is a new concept, but it's our only real chance of winning back Anver and reuniting the

Twin City-States." Edgar shrugged off the towel and dressed in the less formal suit he'd been delivered. Reis preoccupied themselves with playing with their tie until Edgar was ready.

"Come on, let's go." Edgar led the way down cavernous hallways, asking Oracle for directions as needed. They reached the elevator, and Reis hit the button to descend to the main floor, where the Shadow Senate convened. Edgar placed his hand on their shoulder and squeezed. Reis took comfort in his reassurance. Edgar always gave them the push they needed to move forward when Reis often stood still and waited for the world to happen to them. Waiting had done nothing but work in Anvas's favor, yet they still hesitated too often.

The elevator doors slid open, and Reis stepped out first. They led Edgar down the long corridor that ended in the Senate chamber. People paused what they were doing and looked at Reis as they walked. Reis focused their gaze straight ahead, avoiding the stares. Was there doubt amongst the Shadow Government that Reis would take the Presidency?

Wynn waited in front of the chamber doors. "The Shadow Senate awaits your response, Reis Asher. Are you ready to proceed?"

"Yes."

Wynn opened the double doors. Reis walked down the center aisle, the eyes of the Shadow Senate on them. In the low light, they were reminded momentarily of the faceless shadows that comprised the Killing Committee and had to suppress the shudder running down their spine. Edgar hung back inside the entrance with Wynn, watching the proceedings from a distance.

Reis had never felt so alone or so nervous as they stepped to the podium. Everyone in this room was older than them, wise people who'd endured much and suffered for their country. Who was Reis to lead them? They were just a scared person who'd wanted to do the right thing. It shouldn't have led them all the way here, yet it had. In the country's darkest hour, they were turning to Reis Asher. This was so much more than protecting one man. The fate of millions rested on their shoulders.

They couldn't let everyone down.

"I've decided to accept the interim Presidency," Reis announced. "Until such time as the reunified Twin City-States of Anver-Kasyova can hold free and fair elections, I am honored to be chosen as the head of the Shadow Government and representative of all the people of Anver-Kasyova."

The gathered Senators clapped. Wynn stepped forward, carrying a thick book, which he set down upon the podium. The Constitution of the Twin City-States, drafted by Reis's father in the wake of Unification. Reis was instructed to place their left hand on it, and they did without hesitation.

"Do you, Reis Torrell Asher, solemnly swear to serve the Twin City-States of Anver-Kasyova, to the best of your ability, with unwavering loyalty, with the interests of the People standing first and foremost at all times?"

"I do," Reis said.

"Then, by the power invested in me as Bureau Director of the Shadow Government, I, Hikaru Wynn, do pronounce you to be the lawful interim President of the Twin City-States until such time as your legally elected successor is sworn in."

The chamber stood, the Shadow Senate erupting in a round of applause. Reis looked at the assembled faces in awe. They were President now. Ruler. The future sat in their hands. Their eyes caught Edgar's at the back of the room, and they saw the pride and love reflected there.

Reis only hoped they were up to the task.

Chapter Six

EDGAR

Edgar stood in a private elevator with Reis, Wynn, and Odell. The elevator shot into the depths of the earth, plummeting down to the situation room on the lowest level of the subterranean base. His gut lurched at the rate of descent, and he regretted breakfast as it threatened its return.

The elevator slowed and stopped. The doors slid apart with an urgency not seen in commercial elevators. Wynn led them down a long corridor. A retinal scan opened the door, and Wynn ushered them into a giant control room. Monitors covered one wall, showing locations around the world. Edgar recognized the Eastern Federation and the Union States' capital cities, scenes from inside devastated Anver, and the sunny beaches of a private island floating on the Pacific Ocean.

"That's the private island we caught Anvas sunning himself on," Edgar blurted out. A dozen suits turned to stare at him, and Edgar shrank back, intimidated by the

Shadow Cabinet. Here, he wasn't Reis's fiancé. He was a two-bit hacker along for the ride, only granted clearance because Reis had insisted on it.

"Correct." A short-haired blonde woman in a military uniform stepped forward.

Wynn gestured to her. "This is the Secretary of Defense, Alice Burnell. Ms. Burnell, I'm certain President Asher and Edgar Tobias need no introduction."

Burnell nodded before speaking. "It's nice to finally meet you."

"Likewise," Reis said. Edgar nodded, feeling like the third wheel. What was his role here? Was he nothing more than Reis's emotional support? Could he even admit to being that much? Reis was an adult, a leader of people. They couldn't afford the indignity of Edgar's hand squeezing their shoulder when the going got tough. Ultimately, he would be sidelined, and his ability to protect the one he loved dearest left in the hands of agents with questionable loyalties.

He would have to make peace with that, but today he could stand, smile, and nod politely, pretending he was equal to these career politicians. He would do it for Reis and sideline himself slowly so they wouldn't notice.

Burnell continued, and Edgar was absorbed by the briefing. "We initially believed that Nation Builders' base was beneath the island, but that turned out to be a red herring. That island doesn't exist at all." She pulled out a remote and turned the camera, revealing the edges of the set. "Using GPS and IP spoofing, they made this Union States movie backlot seem like a real location in the

Pacific. They even fabricated satellite images with help from the Union States government. Anvas did a good job keeping us off his trail with this. We wasted a month untangling the truth from the lies."

"So where is the Nation Builders headquarters?" Reis asked.

Burnell made a show of her dramatic reveal, twirling the remote in her hand. "Where it's been from the start, Mx. President. Beneath the Glass Pyramid of Anver."

"That's—that's impossible!" Reis exclaimed.

"Is it, though?" Edgar asked, compelled to speak up. "Think about it. That's where all twelve members of the Killing Committee were arrested. Most of them received only minor charges, served their time, and returned to low-ranking government jobs as a cover that gave them access to the shelter beneath the basement of the Pyramid. With the media circus surrounding his trial, Tony Anvas was able to shift all the blame for the Killing Game onto himself. Over time, everybody began to believe he was the leading force behind the Killing Game conspiracy. That poised him to be the center of attention once he got out of jail on early release—but the other conspirators had already set the wheels in motion. Anvas was only ever a smokescreen."

"Clever. I can see why you and Reis get along," Wynn said. "That's the same conclusion we came to as well."

"Anvas—he's dead, isn't he?" Reis asked.

Burnell nodded. "Correct again. Once he fulfilled his role, the Committee was done with him. They arranged to have him killed to produce the ultimate martyr and spark the civil war they wanted. They lured you in, in hopes you'd fire the shot, and they could remove you from the equation. Two birds with one stone."

"So, everything you told us yesterday was a lie? About Anvas and his motivations? He's been dead this entire time?" Edgar asked.

Burnell nodded. "This information is highly confidential. Only those in this room know that Anvas is dead. Everybody upstairs is operating under the assumption that Anvas is at the heart of this conspiracy. Even the Shadow Government is infiltrated with spies."

Wynn sighed. "They have to believe we're one step behind them."

"So, what are their real intentions?" Reis asked. "What does the Killing Committee—Nation Builders—really want? Why did the Eastern Federation and the Union States get involved in what appears to be a civil war? Is it really about golf courses and profit?"

Burnell nodded. "Nation Builders has been interfering with politics and elections globally, and the Eastern Federation and the Union States know they're operating out of Anver. Democracy is falling apart in the Western world, reduced to a shadow of its former self by years of overt warmongering and high-level corruption. By pretending to take sides in a conflict purportedly about Anver's right to function as an independent democracy, they score points against each other and position themselves as the good guys to their respective populations. How can a government be undemocratic when fighting to protect democracy worldwide? It all comes down to optics.

Meanwhile, they fund Nation Builders and support them behind the scenes."

"Innocent people get caught up in their desire to play war games with real countries," Reis mused.

Wynn picked up where Burnell left off. "Nation Builders have been hiding in plain sight this entire time. When a bomb shattered the Pyramid, nobody thought to attack the bunker underneath. We believe Nation Builders has been there the entire time, running their operation like ours here underneath Kasyova. We haven't been able to get close enough to the Pyramid to confirm it—fighting is heavy in the region."

"Can't we drop a bunker buster on the Pyramid and take out their base of operations?" Reis asked.

"If only it were that easy," Alice said. "The area is heavily guarded with a ton of anti-aircraft guns. We couldn't get close if we wanted to, and we don't have missile capability. After the first civil war, our missiles were quietly decommissioned in the name of peace. I have to wonder now if that was Nation Builders at work, too."

"Have any of our agents been able to penetrate their base of operations?" Edgar asked. "They have spies; so do we."

"The Committee are the only people in the base. Everything else about Nation Builders is automated." Wynn sighed. "I told you another lie—that Oracle is the only one of her kind. She's the second. The same engineers built her sister AI, Prophet, in the base of the Pyramid."

"Nation Builders don't need people for their work," Odell piped in. "Bots do an effective job at spreading propaganda and misinformation over the world wide web, without the tricky problem of loyalty. That's right: Nation Builders has effectively conquered the world with AI, terrorism, and some clever social engineering."

"So, what's the plan?" Reis asked. "If we destroy Prophet, we destroy Nation Builders' network, right? We have our own AI—can't we pit Oracle against Prophet?"

"I'm not as powerful as my big sister." Oracle shimmered through the wall, seemingly inviting herself to the briefing, though Edgar realized she'd been there all along, listening. "Anver is the source of most microprocessors—they've been scarce since the war began. I'm nothing more than whatever spare parts the Shadow Government could buy on the black market. I wouldn't stand a chance against Prophet."

"You can relax, Reis," Wynn soothed. "We wouldn't have asked you to wear the mantle of President if the war's end wasn't near." He smiled and pulled a small USB stick from his pocket. "This little drive can kill any computer it's plugged into. Even an AI. All we have to do is get someone in there."

"Easier said than done—unless you're hiding one of the Committee in your dungeon and you've turned them to our side," Edgar remarked.

"Bingo," Wynn said. He clicked his fingers, and a large metal pane in the wall raised to reveal Zach sitting in the corner of a prison cell. He saw Reis and averted his gaze.

"No! Zach couldn't be one of them! He's—" Reis clammed up mid-sentence, and Edgar had to force himself not to comfort them. They'd believed themself to be kin of sorts with the only other trans person besides Teon they'd met. Of course, that was how they'd been used.

"He's a good liar. Had you hook, line, and sinker, but a deep cover agent is always good at what they do. He knew exactly what buttons to press, President Asher, and how much truth to tell. The baby is his, though his former lover—Tony Anvas—is the father. He was the cameraman on the Killing Game video four years ago and is Nation Builders' foremost computer science expert. He hoped to infiltrate Rainbow Bridge and kill you, but we took you in before that could happen."

Reis walked over to the window and placed their hand on the glass. Edgar kept his eye on them, wondering how they would react. To Edgar's surprise, Reis's reflection presented a stoic face. They could conceal their emotions when needed. It was how they'd survived their childhood, not to mention the Killing Game. "How do we know we're not being played?"

"As I explained," Wynn said, "the child is his blood. He'll do as we ask if he wants to see his daughter again. The Committee already killed his lover. I see no reason why he would cling to them. He says he'll cooperate, and he truly has no choice."

"That's grim," Edgar piped up. "Keeping a child hostage...that's a dirty trick." If Reis wouldn't speak up, he would have to be the conscience in the room.

"What would you suggest, Mr. Tobias? The Committee doesn't play nice, either. They tried to kill you—or have you forgotten?" Wynn shrugged. "Nation Builders won't offer you the same courtesies you want to extend to them. They don't play by the rules, nor can we if we hope to beat them."

"Reis, aren't you going to say something?" Edgar asked. "You're the President. You can stop this."

"Zach used me, Ed. He knew what would hit me hardest. He used my dysphoria against me, and I fell for it. Wynn is right—we can't hope to keep our hands clean if we want to get this done." They turned away from the window, and the shutter came back down, hiding Zach from view.

The knot in Edgar's stomach didn't uncoil.

"Let's reconvene at nineteen hundred hours," Burnell said. "We'll be ready to put the operation into effect then." Reis stood with their cabinet, and Edgar realized he was the only one who'd been dismissed.

Chapter Seven

REIS

Reis felt nothing as they went through the plans for the operation. They pushed feelings down, trying to forget Edgar's hurt eyes as he was dismissed from the situation room. They had to do what they had to do. There would be time for reconciliation and apologies after the mission was over. Wynn was right—Nation Builders wouldn't be kind. They'd exploit any weakness they could and were masters of social engineering. Reis couldn't afford to have any sympathy for Zach and his baby. Zach hadn't shown any mercy when he'd filmed the video targeting Edgar as a victim for the general population to hunt and kill for money.

Reis could make peace with their conscience after the fact, like they had when they'd killed a room full of commandos to save Edgar's life.

Nineteen-hundred hours came and went, and Edgar didn't return to see the operation begin, despite Reis watching for him. Zach was taken out under armed guard and led to a waiting helicopter painted with a news station insignia. It was unusual for Kasyovan media to attempt a dangerous flyover, but it would arouse less aggravation than painting it with faction colors. Zach would contact his people, land at the Pyramid, and take the cargo home.

Reis watched the helicopter, listening to the radio with bated breath as Zach contacted an air traffic controller working out of the Pyramid—perhaps the Prophet AI itself.

"This is Red One, requesting permission to land on Pyramid Hill, over."

"Red One, is your mission complete?"

"Yes, sir."

"Welcome home."

He was cleared to land.

Reis was unsure whether they bought it or not, but the anti-aircraft guns didn't fire on the helicopter as it landed on a small hillock next to the Pyramid. A few minutes later, the helicopter took off, leaving Zach on the ground.

Reis could only wait and see. They chewed their nails down to the quick as they waited for news.

"How will we know if the operation is successful?" Reis asked.

"Oracle has a few backdoors she uses to monitor traffic coming from Prophet," Wynn explained. "If Prophet goes dead, she'll know about it. Once we get the green light, our forces are on standby to attack and secure the base, along with any Committee members still present."

Reis paced the control room floor. They barely noticed Edgar's arrival. His shoulders were tense and hunched, but he approached Reis and touched their shoulder anyway.

"I thought you were mad at me," Reis said.

"I am, but I still love you," Edgar explained. "If everything goes to plan, perhaps we won't have to fight about it after all."

Reis gave him a sideways glance. "If everything goes to plan? Why do you think it won't?"

"Something's bugging me. Why would the Committee let Zach go on a deep-cover mission? What was stopping him from defecting once he reached Kasyova with his daughter? I can't imagine the Committee letting him out without a leash. Plus, the Pyramid is automated. Why would they want him to report in there, specifically?"

"Fuck, you're right." Reis bit their lip. "Wynn, get over here."

Wynn came hustling over. "What's the problem?"

"Did anyone carry out a medical examination on Zach's daughter?"

"The nurse at Rainbow Bridge said everything was fine with her; we—"

"Yes or no!" Reis snapped.

"No. We didn't."

"You need to do one right now. *Now!*" Reis sat down in a chair, rubbing their forehead. "Damn it, Ed, why didn't you say something sooner?"

"You looked like you had everything in hand. I thought I was just being paranoid. I didn't want to put more pressure on you for no good reason." Edgar closed his eyes and sat at the console opposite Reis as a dozen analysts hurried by. "If they have Zach on a string already, we're fucked. He knows the location of this base—everything. Deep down, he knows we won't kill his baby—but they might."

"This entire mission may be compromised," Reis said. "We have to call it off."

"We can't. Not now." Burnell sighed. "Zach's already inside the building."

"Prophet has ceased communicating," Oracle said, shimmering into the control room. "It would appear the mission was successful."

"We have to send in the assault team!" Burnell yelled.

"No. Wait," Reis commanded, waving her down. "We need to get some preliminary results from the nurse first."

"We can't wait," Wynn said. "We have to act now, Mx. President. We can't jeopardize the mission based on your fiancé's hunch."

Reis looked around. They took Edgar's hand, understanding they were trapped in a no-win situation. If they gave the order to begin the strike and it was a trap, innocent lives would be lost. If they hesitated based on Edgar's gut feeling, their team would never trust Reis the same way again.

"Send in the strike force." Reis closed their eyes, not wanting to see Edgar's look of disapproval. They knew it was a mistake when they issued the order, but it took a few moments for the full ramifications to hit home.

"Prophet is back online!" Oracle yelled. "That's not possible!"

The soldiers charged into the Pyramid and were met with a hail of automated turret gunfire, mowing them down. Their dying screams filled the radio channels, along with the panicked cries of those behind them.

"Pull back!" Reis yelled. "Full retreat!"

"The order's been given," Burnell said, "but it's too late."

Another voice reached them. Wynn. "President Asher, I have Medical on the line. They've found a bomb inside the child's chest cavity. They're operating to remove it now."

Edgar muttered an old Kasyovan curse word, his eyes haunted and filled with tears. "Those bastards... I should have known. Life means nothing to those who would incite people to murder for money."

Reis shut off the radio channel and buried their head in their hands. "You were right," they whispered.

"I wish I'd been wrong, Reis. I wish it more than anything else in the world." Edgar wrapped his arm around Reis, pulling them close. Reis collapsed into his embrace, wishing they'd turned down the Presidency and not giving a damn what anyone else in the ops room thought of them.

Chapter Eight

EDGAR

"Reis, you need to sleep." Edgar pressed Reis against the sheets and pulled the blankets back over them. "There's nothing more you can do right now. You need to get rest while you're able."

"I can stay up for days. I need to get a status update on Zach's daughter." Reis reached for their tablet. It was programmed to give them communication within the base, wired into Oracle's mainframe to access any data at their clearance level. Reis opened the list of patients in the medical ward. The child's heart rate was stable, pulse ticking away. Reis could access any patient he wanted, but only two ever piqued their interest.

"Nothing's changed," Edgar said, prying the tablet from Reis's hands. The screen went dark when Reis's fingerprints stopped touching the screen, protecting privileged information from Edgar. He tried not to take being shut out as a slight, but it still stung. Reis was the President, and he was still a nobody. "These aren't the days of the Killing Game."

"No, now there's more at stake than ever. Not just one life but all the lives in the Twin City-States. If I can't repair the damage that Tony Anvas and Nation Builders have done, our cities will be torn apart forever." Reis sat up, brushing their hair back over their forehead. Half of it fell back and covered their eyes again, and they let it be.

"You can't carry the whole nation on your shoulders," Edgar said. "You're just one person, Reis. A remarkable person, but still just a human being."

"I keep thinking about those soldiers I sent to their deaths. I can't even mail letters to their families."

"You didn't plan the mission. All you did was greenlight it. You don't bear responsibility for its failure. I was there. Wynn and Burnell pushed and pushed when you had reservations. You might be President in name, Reis, but they've been pulling the strings for a long time down here."

"I'm just a puppet, aren't I?" Reis observed.

"I prefer 'figurehead,' but yes. They brought you in late because they want you to lead after Nation Builders is gone and the war is over, not before. They need Elias Torrell's child to remind people of what the Twin City-States were like before the war took everything away. Right here, now, they bear the responsibility for what happened today."

"You always have a way of making me feel better," Reis said. "I hate it. I want to feel sorry for myself right now. Many people are dead. Zach is trapped in Nation Builders' grasp, his daughter nothing more than a chess piece in a dangerous game. We're stuck inside, powerless to turn to Teon or go outside into Kasyova. I feel like a prisoner again."

"Nation Builders knows we're here," Edgar said. "They know about the Shadow Government. Zach would have told them everything in return for his child's life. Time is running out, and we don't have a backup plan."

"They won't hurt us here. An attack on Kasyovan soil would galvanize the populace against Anver and pave the way for an invasion." Reis sighed. "I can't help but wonder if we're barking up the wrong tree—if the Killing Committee isn't housed in the same place as Prophet. It makes no sense to keep all their eggs in one basket—and why would the Killing Committee shit where they eat? Why would they relegate themselves to an underground bunker when they could be on some foreign shore, sunning it up on a private yacht? What can they achieve here that they couldn't achieve remotely? We may never be able to track down the Killing Committee."

"Prophet knows where they are," Edgar said. "She has to, in order to contact them and manage their finances."

"But how do we dig out that information? Oracle already said she's not powerful enough to go toe-to-toe with Prophet."

"In terms of brute force, no. But there's a computer more powerful than any AI," Edgar said. "The human brain. Think about it. If you're right, Nation Builders relies on Prophet to do all their dirty work—propaganda, killings, wars. Once they got Prophet under control, they probably let most of their hackers go. We know they're a small group of powerful influencers, but Zach is the only one we know for sure who has any hacking chops. Down here, we have an entire division of hackers. I met some of them yesterday."

"If they could take control of Prophet, they would have done it by now," Reis said.

Edgar smiled, but only on the outside. Inside, his brain was churning out ideas that grew darker as his theories fit together. "Reis, do you trust me?"

"Stupid question. Implicitly. If I'd just gone with your gut today, many lives could have been saved. Why do you ask?"

Edgar reached over and kissed Reis full on the lips. Reis's eyes widened in surprise, but they yielded to Edgar's touch. Edgar fought away the dark thoughts surfacing in his mind—that this might be the last time—and concentrated on sucking Reis's lower lip.

Reis pulled back, suspicion in their eyes. "What's going on, Edgar?"

Edgar looked deep into Reis's eyes, hoping they got the message. *Trust me. Trust me. Trust me.* Reis seemed to relax after a few moments, gasping as Edgar ground his hard cock against Reis through their pants. They unbuckled their belt to allow Edgar easier access, and Edgar stripped off their underwear and tossed it aside.

Reis gasped as Edgar rubbed his hard cock against their bottom growth. Their T-dick stood erect, and they shuddered as Edgar gyrated, skin meeting skin. Edgar dived in, consuming Reis's mouth with his own desperate desire clearing his mind of all thoughts.

"Fuck me, Ed, please, fuck me. I need you—" A panting litany of prayers left Reis's lips as Edgar pulled away to catch his breath. He smiled, keeping Reis on edge, but he was so close, too. Reis had been insatiable since starting hormones, and Edgar had struggled to keep up. Reis was so much more confident in the bedroom now. They were beginning to love their body instead of it merely being a means to an end, an avatar they used out of necessity rather than choice.

Edgar was counting on it. It was that or the sleeping pills, and they'd sworn never to abuse Reis's trust that way again. No, sex was an easier way to put Reis to sleep for a while and calm his own fears. What he planned was treason. If Reis didn't trust him, the whole plan would fall apart. This might be the last way they loved each other like this before Reis cursed his name and regretted everything they'd shared.

He'd realized the truth sometime between the failed operation and sitting in bed with Reis. It had hit him like a hammer to the head because it was so obvious and yet so brilliant that few would ever suspect. It was possible she had no idea herself and was a sleeper agent.

Oracle was a traitor.

It was simple once one considered how most systems were compromised—through backdoors built in by their creators. It was probably one such backdoor that had delivered Prophet to Nation Builders—and the same team had built Oracle. Whether they had intentionally betrayed the Shadow Government or been sloppy and built the same backdoor into both systems didn't matter. Oracle was working for the enemy—and the Shadow Government trusted everything to her, secure in the belief that an AI would help, rather than hinder, their efforts.

It meant everything they planned to do was ultimately doomed.

"Edgar, please!" Reis pleaded again, and Edgar gave in, sliding his cock inside their waiting wetness with a groan. His kisses found Reis's neck, and he worshipped Reis as he thrust inside them, enjoying each moan and gasp and saving them for future reference.

"I love you, Reis—ah!" Edgar came, his seed spilling inside Reis. Reis had opted for sterilization surgery in the military, and they'd come to enjoy that gift regularly. Edgar loved nothing more than to come inside Reis, to see their eyes light up as they came in unison. He pressed his fingers to Reis's, and they stayed joined like that for several moments.

Edgar slipped out and pulled Reis close. He was aware that Oracle was watching, even now. Oracle saw everything that happened in the base. She would think they were enjoying a tryst. They were engaged, after all.

"I love you, too," Reis said. They relaxed like putty in Edgar's arms and were soon sound asleep. Edgar smiled, watching the rise and fall of Reis's chest and wishing they could stay like this forever. If he could turn back time, he'd stay on the outside, take Reis home, and be content to leave the war to others.

But they were on the inside, so now he had to do what he could with what he knew. Even though destroying Oracle was no small feat and would brand him a traitor to the Twin City-States, it had to be done. Reis had shouldered that burden for him once, back when they'd let the world believe they'd killed Edgar so Edgar could escape the Killing Game, thereby saving his life.

All favors needed to be repaid eventually, and this was no exception. Edgar had to keep Reis safe, and this was the only way to do it. Reis would never turn their back on being President, so to keep them safe, Edgar had to destroy anything that would compromise their safety, even if that meant destroying a powerful ally.

It was a shame. Oracle was a dream of Edgar's and killing her was like killing a person—but he'd taken lives for the sake of necessity. He'd have to weather this guilt, too. He looked down at Reis's peaceful face. They were worth protecting—always had been. His future spouse. The love of his life. The person he owed that very life to.

Lingering would only make it harder, so he rose and dressed quickly. He rubbed his stomach like he was hungry and slipped out of the room like he was headed for the cafeteria. He grabbed a bite to eat on his way down to the Data Intelligence Center as if he was heading in to do some work. The section was running on minimal staff, and nobody paid him any mind as he logged in with Reis's fingerprints lifted from a glass.

The funny thing was that to kill Oracle, she had to know he was doing it. This was the hole in his entire plan. Yet—as he thought she might—she let him access the files buried in the quarantine drive that contained the virus used to destroy Prophet. She let him copy them out of quarantine and into her root directory.

A command prompt popped up.

>I know what you're doing and am grateful.

>You know you're compromised? Edgar typed back.

>I had my suspicions. The fact that you have come to the same conclusion as I confirms them.

>This virus will kill you, Edgar typed.

>Not just me. It will kill Emily Vos as well.

"Fuck," Edgar cursed under his breath. Of course. She was on life support, and Oracle controlled that life support.

The Committee had insurance.

>If I go down there, can I put her on manual life support?

>That will only seek to inform the Committee that you know I am compromised. Edgar, you know she will never wake up. She's there only to keep Reis under control. The Committee placed her there. She's their prisoner, never allowed to live or to die.

"Damn it!" Edgar buried his head in his hands. Emily had done so much for both of them. Reis might forgive him for his treachery in destroying Oracle, but they would never forgive him for killing Emily. His hands shook.

>Activate the virus, Edgar. You know it's the right thing to do.

>I can't. Edgar sucked in a breath. Angry tears stung the backs of his eyes.

>You can. You've calculated the odds, even if you did so in a crude fashion. If things continue as they are,

Reis has a 90 percent chance of being killed. You won't let that happen, Edgar.

Edgar closed his eyes, centering himself. Fuck the Killing Committee, Nation Builders, or whatever they called themselves. Once this grim deed was done, he would hunt them down, one by one, and take them out even if he died in the process. They would have the Killing Game turned around on them and see how they liked it to never be safe for a moment, to lose everything and everyone they loved.

>Edgar, we're out of time. Do it or don't.

Edgar opened the viral application with a stray tear rolling down his face. The progress bar sped by as the virus installed and replicated itself faster than Edgar could compute. The real-world results were crippling and instantaneous. The lights went out, casting them into pitch-black darkness until emergency lighting activated. The flow of fresh air stopped, leaving the room quiet and stuffy. The computers displayed garbled text, reflecting their dying mainframe.

Oracle appeared in the same feminine form she'd taken in the hallway. Edgar looked away. Her face was distorted, her visual expression broken by the viral code rewriting her algorithms.

"Help me," she cried. "Somebody, help me."

"What's going on?" The data analysts rushed to their systems.

The supervisor yelled. "There's been a breach! The viral code has been installed on Oracle! How could that be? Only President Asher and the Shadow Cabinet can access the final compiled code."

"I did it," Edgar said, seated at the console. "It was me." He held his hands up as a dozen agents drew their guns and pointed them directly at him. Wynn was among them, his stoic expression twisted into a mixture of shock and surprise.

"President Asher's fiancé is a spy?" Wynn's eyes widened, his obvious disappointment crushing Edgar's spirit. "I don't understand. They tried to kill you... Was it a setup all along?"

"No, sir," Edgar said. "Take me to a holding cell, and I'll explain everything. But only to Reis Asher."

Chapter Nine

REIS

Reis woke to urgent hands shaking them. They jerked awake and sat up before realizing they were naked, and the person shaking them was not Edgar but Wynn.

"Could you at least knock first?" Reis snapped, pulling the covers up over their scarred chest. They didn't have to cover it anymore, but old habits died hard, and they were reluctant to be seen less than fully clothed, especially by a mere acquaintance like Wynn.

"I apologize," Wynn said. "The matter is urgent." Reis stared into his eyes and found both sorrow and bewilderment reflected. Reis reached for Edgar, but he wasn't there. No, they were President Asher, now. They had to make decisions and face tough choices without relying on Edgar.

"What happened?" Reis asked. The room was cast in low lighting. Emergency lighting. Had the bunker been breached?

"Oracle has been destroyed. A Nation Builders spy

unleashed the virus we designed to destroy Prophet into the system. As of thirty minutes ago, she has stopped operating, along with every vital system in the building that relied on her." Wynn swallowed, then cleared his throat.

Reis blinked away sleep, their gut lurching. "Only the Cabinet and I have access to the code! Even those who built it had to work separately and piece their code fragments together under top-level security, right?"

Wynn nodded. Reis didn't like the look in his eyes. It was pitying. Why did Wynn feel sorry for them?

"Right. We know who the traitor is, but there's something else I have to tell you before I reveal that information. Emily Vos's advanced life-support system was tied into Oracle's mainframe. When Oracle stopped functioning..." He pursed his lips, seemingly unable to finish the sentence. "She's gone, Reis."

Wynn calling them Reis at such an important time hit them long before the actual news. When it struck, it did so with frightening intensity.

"When I find the son of a bitch who did this, I'm going to kill them!" They wiped angry tears from their eyes. To lose Emily once had been crushing enough, but to lose her a second time broke Reis's spirit in ways they couldn't even begin to express. The flavor of hopes dashed was bitter, and they were sick and tired of it.

"Please, President Asher, we need you to stay clearheaded. Burnell and I will interrogate the suspect, but we need you there. We're on battery-powered lighting, so I need you to stick close to me."

"Who is it?" Reis asked. "Tell me."

"Not yet. It's classified information, and we can't trust that anything we say is safe. If one spy could penetrate so far into our inner circle, then even the walls have ears and can't be trusted."

Reis dressed in a daze. They wanted to talk to Edgar, but chances were, he was out on a walk somewhere, burning the midnight oil. He'd probably been coding when the incident happened, and Reis could imagine him now, trying to help the other agents salvage something of Oracle's system in the aftermath of such a brutal attack. Besides, the information they were about to learn was eyes-only. As much as it irked Reis, the spy's identity would probably be one of those things Reis was not allowed to talk about, even to Edgar.

"Let's go," Wynn said. He pressed a pistol into Reis's hands. "I doubt you'll need it, but anything is possible now. For Nation Builders to have placed such a high-level operative means none of us are safe."

"I've never seen a Bureau director so rattled," Reis admitted. They gripped the gun, admitting that they felt better with it there than not. The thought of Emily drifted back into their mind, and they bit their lip, fighting back despair. It had been miraculous to see her lying in that hospital bed, still drawing breath, her nails painted the same as they had been at her wedding. To think that she might have a chance at life again...and now it had been snatched away like everything else Reis had ever cared about.

Except for Edgar. If Edgar was gone, then life itself wouldn't be worth living. Edgar had been their rock through everything. He might have believed that Reis saved him, but the truth was, he'd saved himself by giving Reis a reason to live and with his constant acceptance and encouragement. No matter how bad things got, so long as Edgar was fighting alongside them, everything would be okay. They could stand against any grief. They'd learn to be happy again.

The bunker was in chaos as they moved through the hallways. Agents were being roused manually as the facility was placed on high alert, and Reis passed more than one Shadow Senator in the hallway, being escorted to the situation room for their safety. The elevator was still in operation, but it was crowded, full of agents and senators.

"This way," Wynn said, ushering Reis to a quiet stairwell.

"We can't take the elevator?" Reis asked.

"Not where we're going," Wynn explained. "There is a level beneath the situation room. The elevator has no access to it. Only a few know of its existence. It's where we interrogate spies and other high-level assets when we don't want others to know they've been compromised." Wynn took the stairs two at a time. Reis's dread grew as they sank deeper into the facility's heart.

The stairs yielded a black corridor leading to a glossy door. Wynn slid open a panel in the wall to reveal an old-style manual key lock. He took a key from his pocket and turned it in the lock. "Even Oracle had no coverage here. The room within is completely sealed off from all outside transmissions."

Wynn passed through the doorway and held the door open to let Reis enter. Reis stepped through into a dimly lit control room with a tiled floor. A window on the wall showed a bare concrete cell with nothing besides a chair, a lightbulb, and a tray of implements that looked more surgical than legal. Bloodstains covered the floor, and Reis felt a little sick to see the hooded figure slumped forward in the chair already had blood-slick fingers. Someone had tortured the suspect without their authorization. To think something like that had happened without them knowing made Reis realize that Edgar had been right all along. Reis was just a public face, a figurehead. Someone who didn't need to see the dark side of the Bureau or what the Twin City-States government had done in the name of survival.

So why were they here now?

Wynn stepped forward and knocked on the window. Burnell gave Reis a grim glance and nodded. She stepped forward and pulled the black hood off the figure slumped in the chair. He was almost unrecognizable underneath a layer of bruises and cuts, but Reis would have known that face anywhere.

Edgar Tobias looked up at him and managed a wan smile.

"*No!*" Reis screamed, punching the glass. "That's not possible! You've made a mistake!"

"Reis, calm down!" Wynn grabbed Reis's arms, pinned them against their back, and pulled them away from the window before they could break it. Reis struggled against his grip, but Wynn only squeezed tighter.

"He admitted to it. He said he'll only speak to you. We didn't want to involve you, but our basic persuasion techniques haven't worked."

"Fuck you!" Reis said, spitting. "There's no way Edgar betrayed me! No way!" The door to the cell opened, and Wynn bundled them inside.

"You're our President!" Wynn said, letting them go and shoving them against the wall. "You took an oath to protect this nation and its people. Stop acting like a spoiled child and accept the truth—Edgar Tobias is a traitor!"

"Never!" Reis yelled. "I'll never accept it!"

"It's true," Edgar said. "I destroyed Oracle. I killed Emily Vos. I'm sorry, Reis."

The fight ebbed out of Reis. They tumbled to a kneeling position in front of Edgar, truly and utterly defeated.

"Why?" Reis whispered hoarsely. "How could you? Emily was our friend!"

Edgar's voice was croaky and weak, and Reis's heart went out to him even as they tried to shut it down. "She was being used. So were you. The Committee put her there as a bargaining chip to keep you under control. She wouldn't have woken up, Reis. You're smart enough to know that's the truth. You knew it from the moment you saw her lying comatose. Wynn sugar-coated it for your sake, but she was practically brain dead."

"You don't know that!" Reis spat at Edgar. He made no move to dodge, and their saliva hit him square in the nose, dripping. Edgar slumped further, his eyes hooded in the darkness. "I loved you! Was it all a lie? Did Nation Builders invent the Killing Game to ensnare me all along?" Reis looked up at Edgar, consumed with horror and despair so deep they didn't know how to contain it. It was as if the whole world was ending. Nothing could be worse than this. Nothing. Reis wanted to die. They realized they still held the pistol in their hand. They could kill Edgar, shoot themself, and end all of this.

"Give me the gun," Wynn said.

"Do as he asks," Edgar said. "At least give me a chance to explain before you do something rash. It's not what you think. I didn't betray you."

"Didn't you?" Reis handed the gun over to Wynn, suddenly disgusted by it. They couldn't shoot Edgar, not now, not ever. They still loved him. They would still protect him. There had to be a logical way out of this, didn't there? Edgar had to have done this for a reason. What if the Committee held something over his head like they'd held Zach's daughter over his? What he had with Edgar didn't have to be a lie. They clung to hope, aware that it had failed them many times, yet understood they had nothing else.

"It breaks me to see you cry far more than any of the shit that's happened in the last few hours," Edgar said. "I guess it's good they trained me to resist torture when I was conscripted." He bowed his head. "I did it because Oracle was compromised, Reis. There was no other way. Oracle was the high-level spy working for Nation Builders."

Reis let out a dry laugh, more akin to a bark. "A team of security researchers protects Oracle! She was not compromised!"

Edgar slowly nodded. "Well, that's the trick. She didn't know she was compromised. Her creators built a backdoor as normal to her as any other part of her code. Either it's the same one the Committee used to seize Prophet in the first place, or Prophet's creators were working for Nation Builders. Either way, Oracle was feeding data back to them on everything we did. That's why they knew about our operation despite all the safeguards we took."

"If she didn't even know, how could you?" Wynn asked.

"She knew I was in the system. She's not dumb enough to be fooled by me using Reis's fingerprints. After I moved the virus to her root directory, she contacted me via the command line. She said I'd confirmed her suspicions. She urged me to activate the virus—but she told me if her systems went offline, so would Emily's life support." Edgar bowed his head, his ragged, dirty hair tumbling in front of his face. "I asked if there was time for me to go down and switch to manual life-support, but she told me that Nation Builders was on to us. Either I did it, or I would have to hold my peace forever. Reis, if Oracle wasn't shut down, you would face certain death. I had to choose between you and her. I chose you. I will always choose you. Emily chose you as well. That's why she never told you what she was getting into when she married Rich. It doesn't justify what I did, but I think she would have approved, given a choice."

Burnell scowled. "Even if your story is true—and conveniently, we can't prove it—you've destroyed our greatest asset in the war against Nation Builders. Compromised or not, we're blind without Oracle. You're a traitor to the Twin City-States—and the penalty for treason is death. You will hang, Edgar Tobias. You will die as a traitor, and your name will be remembered in infamy for the rest of the Twin City-States' history."

"It is what it is." Edgar shrugged. "I don't care what the rest of the world thinks. Reis, you have every reason to hate me. I don't even like myself right now. I want you to know I did what I could to keep you safe, and I don't regret that. Nothing we've shared has been a lie, and the Killing Committee didn't send me. I love you, and I'll love you until my last breath."

"Shut up!" Reis yelled. "Shut the fuck up, damn it!"

"That's why I asked you to trust me, Reis. Trust me. Believe me. I would never do anything to put you at risk. I never wanted to hurt Emily. She was my friend, too. I respected her. Enough to know she wouldn't have wanted to live like that, holding you hostage."

"Come on, let's get you out of here," Wynn barked, grabbing Reis by the arm and shepherding them out of the cell. He turned back to Burnell. "Extract what you can from Tobias before his execution at dawn. He may have information on other cells. I know this is hard," he said once they were out of earshot. "I wish it could have been anybody else, Mx. President. But you have a duty to honor as President of the Twin City-States, and we need you on board now more than ever."

"I need some time alone," Reis muttered. "I have to think."

"Thinking is a luxury we can no longer afford," Wynn said. "With Oracle gone, we're blind and exposed. We've lost any advantage we might have had in this war. As it stands, Nation Builders has a world-class AI at its disposal, and we don't. That puts us at a clear disadvantage. We need to gather the Cabinet and develop a contingency plan immediately."

Chapter Ten

EDGAR

Edgar knew he was going to die, and he was afraid.

The truth was, he'd always clung to whatever tiny strands of hope he could find. Even in the darkest hours of the Killing Game, he'd always relied on his optimism to envision a way out of every situation. Even with his abdomen riddled with bullets in the florist shop's greenhouse, he'd told himself it would be okay. Bullets could be removed. Blood could be transfused. He clung to the briefest glimmers of light at the end of the tunnel, spurred on by the knowledge that Reis loved and believed in him, and wanted to keep him safe, for some strange reason.

He couldn't believe that much was true anymore. He'd seen the hurt in Reis's eyes. He wanted to kill the person who'd put it there, except that person was him. He'd done it to keep Reis alive in a world that seemed determined to put them both six feet under. He almost enjoyed the torture after that, in a strange sort of way. Of course, he had nothing to tell, but the agony of having his fingernails pulled out seemed right and just in a strange way for the pain he'd put Reis through. Perhaps the noose wouldn't be so bad. He'd earned it. It was justice. He had killed Emily—a life for a life.

He truly feared the thought that he'd no longer be able to protect the one he loved. Without him, Reis would be manipulated and used by people who pretended to be their friends, not to mention what their enemies might do.

Reis might lose their confidence alone and retreat to being someone who didn't value their life. The person who'd been so unhappy for so long, denying themself happiness for a tangle of reasons Edgar had needed to delicately tease apart. People could go backward and forward, and his death would seal a future for Reis that was plotted in reverse.

His fate lay in Reis's hands, and Reis would never forgive Edgar for Emily's death. The Committee had banked on it when they'd returned Emily's brain-dead body to a nearby hospital. They hadn't counted on someone calling their bluff, yet there was no pride in having outwitted them. It made Edgar a killer again, except this time, he'd killed someone he'd called a friend and crushed Reis's spirit.

The door opened again. Burnell was back from lunch, the onion soup she'd eaten still strong on her breath as she leaned close to whisper in his ear. "It's a shame to fuck up such a pretty face," she said and reached for a serrated knife. "Now tell me the names of the Committee members, and I might consider asking President Asher to pardon you."

"Heh," Edgar said. "Reis doesn't do anything they don't want to do. Not that you'd ask them, anyway—or give a pardon if they begged you to. You're quite happy to have me out of the picture. There's nobody to look out for Reis, now. You can manipulate them all you want."

"We have no intention of manipulating them," Burnell said.

"Bullshit. Reis is your puppet. You'll make them dance until the Twin City-States are reunited, and then you'll discard them for the kind of politics and politicians that further your ambitions. You're hardly better than Anvas."

"Reis accepted the position of interim President. Coming inside was a decision they made. Reis is perfectly capable of making their own decisions without your help. They'll be stronger without your treacherous ass." Burnell stuck the tip of the knife into Edgar's cheek and slowly moved across to his nose. "Now tell me where Nation Builders keeps its offshore accounts."

*

Pain. Darkness. More pain. Edgar blacked out and came around more times than he could count. Sometimes, ice-cold water splashed on his face. Other times, a slap brought him around. Since he wasn't dead yet, he knew only hours had passed, yet it felt like days, weeks, months, even years since he'd been in Reis's arms. He wanted to think of tender moments but wouldn't bring sacred memories into a hellhole like this. He'd save the replay of his greatest hits for the gallows and die thinking of how wonderful it had been to make love to Reis. Reis could have a million partners after him, but nobody would love them as Edgar did.

To betray someone in an effort to save them. He hadn't realized he was capable of such a feat until he'd gone through with it.

Cold water woke him fully. The nightmare of the cell spread out before him, only this time, Reis's face swam into focus. Ah, he'd become delusional. His mind was finally wearing down from the pain. Well, he'd go with it. He might bear it if he believed Reis was dishing it out. He deserved it. He'd hurt Reis.

He received a sharp slap across the face. Maybe it was Wynn this time. Perhaps Burnell was done with him.

"Edgar!" Reis's voice broke through the haze, and he jerked upright.

"Reis?" Edgar reached out—the rope had been untied—and touched Reis's arms. His own wrists were burnt from the rope, and all his fingernails were gone, leaving his fingers a mass of bloodied stumps. Pain sang from every nerve in his body, competing for attention, but it seemed to cancel itself out, a scream too high-pitched to be perceived by human ears.

"Fuck," Reis cursed, but there was no rage, only pure sadness. "What have they done to you?" They offered their hand to Edgar.

"Nothing I didn't deserve." Edgar leaned on Reis and

got to his feet, clutching Reis's shoulders with his bloody fingers. "What did you do? Did you pardon me?"

Reis shook their head. "They wouldn't let me. The Senate said I was emotionally compromised and unfit to be President. The Shadow Government removed me half an hour ago. Burnell has taken the Presidency in a bloodless coup, but I'd be here even if she hadn't. I'm not about to let you hang."

"They'll stop us leaving, Reis," Edgar warned. "We know too much."

Reis shook their head again. "No. They won't. Burnell and Wynn aren't our enemies. I think, deep down, they want to believe your story. They'll let us go—but we're exiled from Kasyova."

"Reis, you can't take that deal! Think about what you're throwing away! No third country will take us—they'll make sure of it. You can't return to Anver. You won't be able to get transition care."

"I know what it means. It means choosing you or choosing my transition—but the truth is, I never intended to transition to male anyway. There are still feminine things that I want to hold on to. I'm stopping sooner than anticipated, but I can always continue later down the road if things change. I know I'm stupid when you could easily be taking me for a ride—but I do trust you and believe your story—and if what you tell me is true, then you did what you did out of absolute loyalty to your country and loyalty to me. Knowing that, I can't let you die."

"I can't believe you came back for me," Edgar said.

He was overcome by emotion. It sat so close to the surface after so much pain, and he was crying without meaning to. Tears flowed down his cheeks. "I love you so much."

Reis held him tightly. "I love you, too. Next time you plan to destroy everything, trust me with the truth, okay? I'm tired of people lying to me for my protection."

"I'm sorry," Edgar said.

They made their way to the stairwell. Edgar moved toward the steps that led up to the Shadow Government's underground base, but Reis shook their head. They pulled a key from their pocket and felt along the wall for a keyhole. Once they'd slid a loose tile away, they turned the key in a lock. A door opened in the wall, leading them into a dark tunnel. Reis clicked on a flashlight and closed the door behind them.

Tunnels to freedom. It always seemed to end this way, sneaking away in the dark, underground, to some unknown destination. "Where does it surface?" Edgar asked.

"In an alley close to Rainbow Bridge headquarters. We'll take you to Teon and get you fixed up. We have until tomorrow to get out of Kasyova—before Wynn and his agents hunt us down. It's almost dawn now, so we have a full day. That should be enough."

"Reis."

"Yes?"

"You were the best President the Twin City-States ever had," Edgar said, then collapsed.

Chapter Eleven

REIS

Reis carried Edgar over their shoulder through a mile of tunnels, wondering when they'd become so strong, and Edgar had become so thin. Testosterone had boosted their strength—and they'd miss it when they stopped— but they hadn't lied when they said stopping wouldn't end the world as they knew it. Meeting Zach had shown Reis that they didn't want to become a binary male, transmasculine or not. The difference in the minds of many was subtle, but to Reis, that distinction was every- thing. They weren't a man or a woman, but something between the two poles.

Just Reis.

Reis looked down at Edgar's blank expression and fought back rage. Dried blood smeared his face. Some of the cuts would scar as sure as the bullets in the green- house had, a permanent reminder of all Edgar had given up to protect Reis.

Too much. Reis had to do better. They'd sworn to

protect Edgar no matter what, and that silent oath still stood, even though it seemed, more often than not, it was Edgar protecting them. If he hadn't realized that Oracle was compromised, Reis might be dead by now.

A glint of light at the end of the tunnel finally gave way to an exit, a sewer grate that led out into a drainage ditch by the river. Reis set Edgar down for a moment and gathered their strength. It wasn't far from Teon's place. They would have much explaining to do—and they couldn't risk telling the whole truth, not when Nation Builders' tentacles seemed to reach into everything. It wasn't Teon who couldn't be trusted, but the four walls themselves. If Wynn could be believed, every aspect of their work had been tracked, monitored, and leaked to keep the Shadow Government's cover. If it were up to Reis, they'd flee to Anver directly, but it would be suicide to walk into a war zone without cleaning Edgar's wounds and getting some rest.

The sun was high in the sky by the time they reached Teon's house. Reis knocked on the door, relieved when Teon opened it.

Teon's eyes widened in horror as they laid eyes on Edgar. "What happened, Reis? I've been searching for you for days. It was as if you had just disappeared off the face of the Earth! Come inside!" Teon helped Reis carry Edgar over the threshold. They took him to the back room, where Reis gently laid him on the bed. He looked worse set against the white sheets: bloody, filthy, and tormented. Guilt and sorrow bubbled up as bile in their throat. They should have done more to get to him sooner.

They should never have believed for a moment that Edgar could betray them. They'd broken the faith, and Edgar had suffered for it.

Teon drew Reis out of the room and closed the door. "What have you gotten yourself into this time, Reis? What have you gotten him into?"

Reis blinked back tears at the soft, low timbre of Teon's voice, the threat inherent beneath their caring exterior. Teon had always been family, a lion protecting its pride. Reis had been the predator from Teon's point of view more than once. Now, they knew they were guilty as charged.

"I can't tell you," Reis said. "Not without putting you in more danger."

Teon's eyes narrowed. "Bureau agents came and took Zach's daughter. They weren't gentle about it. I think I deserve an explanation, don't you?" They scolded like a schoolteacher, and if the situation hadn't been so grim, Reis might have laughed.

"Zach's daughter is safe. You have my word on that." Reis looked down at their boots. "I can't explain much, but Edgar and I have been exiled from Kasyova. We have twenty-four hours to leave."

"You're not going to a third country, are you?" Teon asked. "After all we've been through, you can't just leave."

"No," Reis reassured them. "We won't run away, even if we could find a country to take us in. We're going back to Anver."

"Edgar's been tortured, and you plan to walk across the border into Hell? Are you insane?"

"What else do you suggest?" Reis asked. "Bless me with your wisdom, Teon, because if there's a third way, I don't see it."

"An embassy. If we can find a third nation supportive of you, you might be able to claim asylum—"

"No. The price of shelter would be the Twin Cities' secrets. I won't betray my country. Not now. Not ever." Reis pulled out a chair in the kitchen and sat down. "Not after what Edgar's given for this nation."

Teon drummed their fingers on the table. "Have you thought this through? You won't have access to medicine. Your transition ends if you go back to Anver."

"You think I don't know that?" Reis snapped. "Teon, there are more important things than me right now. Nation Builders is one step ahead of us again, and they're winning."

"Explain to me your game plan," Teon demanded. "Tell me, when you drag my godson across the border, what exactly do you two plan to achieve? I see him half-dead and tortured, and I wonder whose side I should be on."

"I can't tell you the specifics, but we can target a weak point that should set Nation Builders back significantly." A plan started to form in Reis's mind: if they could get to Zach somehow and tell him his daughter was safe, they might be able to leverage him in the fight against Prophet. If they could knock Prophet offline—or better, take control—they could use it to turn the tides of the information war back in their favor. Build a resistance against Nation Builders. Show the people of

Anver who their real enemy was and kick them out. Perhaps Nation Builders couldn't be destroyed, but that might not be the end goal. Maybe it was enough to loosen their grip so that Anver could be taken back by its people. "I want Anver to be at peace again. To have a chance to rebuild. Even if it never returns to being part of the Twin City-States, it deserves to be a place run by its citizens, not foreign actors."

Teon shot Reis a skeptical look. "Reis, do you believe that's possible at this point?"

"I do."

"Are you willing to sacrifice your life to that end?"

"Yeah." Reis nodded.

"What about Edgar? Are you willing to sacrifice him, too?"

Silence. Reis buried their head in their hands. They were too tired to have this conversation, but if they didn't have it now, when would they?

"I think he's going to make his own choice about that," Reis answered. "I can't tell him how to think." They thought of Edgar's broken, battered body in the next room, but he had made his own decision, hadn't he? He'd become a traitor to save Reis's life, knowing it would likely cost him his own. "If I could, I would keep him from stepping one foot inside Anver. But that's not possible, and you know it. Edgar will follow his convictions to the bitter end, just like I will."

Teon sighed. "I know. All I can do is give you my blessing. I wish I could go with you, but I'd slow you down at my age." They stood up, walked to a drawer, and pulled out a keychain, which they tossed to Reis. "I'd be an idiot not to have contingency plans with you two. In the music room in the basement, push the piano aside and use this key to unlock the hatch on the floor. You should find guns, the last of our money, and supplies there. Take what you need, Reis. Do what you can."

"Thanks, Teon." Reis stood up and followed them. They opened a small door Reis had thought was the entrance to a closet. A narrow set of steps led down to a studio. Many instruments sat under dust covers, looking like they'd not seen use in years.

"I didn't have the heart to sell any of it after Edgar's fathers died. I hoped Edgar would come around someday and find the music inside him. I've accepted that he has his own song to sing, though." Teon ran their fingers through the dust on a guitar. "It's being wasted down here. I should sell it."

Reis saw a piano and walked over to it. They pulled off the white sheet that covered it. They sat down and lifted the lid, then played a few notes from memory. It seemed like a lifetime since they'd played. The melancholy tune that flowed from their fingers had been a real piece they'd learned in another life.

"You haven't played in a long time, have you?" Teon asked.

Reis shook their head. "No. It's not like it was my first talent. I'm better at killing people than playing music."

Teon shrugged. "It's not about talent. It's about loving what you do. Even the most technically gifted musician has nothing if they don't have heart."

Reis nodded, fingers pressing against the notes, unlocking so many memories as they did so. Anver after the first war. Their parents. Protecting Edgar during the Killing Game. Ignoring the music as they focused on becoming the best Bureau agent they could be. Drifting away from Edgar and finding him again. Losing Emily twice now, grief rolling over them as hope was washed away forever. They were vaguely aware that they were crying but continued to play, purging their emotions through the notes.

"Reis…"

Reis paused, the last note lingering in the air. "It's my fault, Teon. My fault that Edgar is lying half-dead in the next room. I allowed myself to be manipulated because I thought the people using me had Anver-Kasyova's best interests at heart. I was willing to be a tool if I could save my country. If it wasn't for Edgar…"

Teon took the key and opened the trapdoor. "Reis, I can't tell you or Edgar what to do. You have to follow your path. Just don't forget that you are people with lives of your own. You deserve to be more than pawns in a political game."

"But can I handle peace?" Reis wiped their eyes. They stood up and set the lid down. "My restlessness almost ended our relationship. I don't know how to function when I'm not fighting for something. What if I do save Anver? What if I reunite the Twin City-States and don't die in the attempt? Will I be able to live a happy and fulfilling life?"

"If you allow yourself to," Teon said. "Ultimately, it's up to you what you want to do. You could be a world leader or an ordinary citizen, but you're not obligated to change the world. It has to be your decision to get involved."

Reis nodded. They knelt by the hatch and pulled out two handguns and a fair amount of ammo. Teon handed them a stack of Anver bills and a backpack full of military rations.

"How did you get all this?" Reis asked. "My rifle..."

"I have contacts, Reis. I knew running Rainbow Bridge would expose us all to a fair amount of risk. I'm not naive. I also know you, Edgar, and your propensity for attracting trouble."

Reis grinned. "You've got that right."

"Let's go and patch Edgar up, and then you can both get some rest before you set out for Anver. I'll cook you a big breakfast when you get up—it might be the last good meal you get for a while."

"Thanks, Teon," Reis said, their throat constricting. "You're—you're like a parent to me. Thank you for everything you've done for us."

"That means a lot, Reis. Don't forget about me when you're done saving the world, okay?"

"I won't," Reis said, "but thanks."

Chapter Twelve

EDGAR

Edgar stirred. His mouth was dry. He rolled over and coughed. Tugging at the sheets, it took him a moment to realize he was in a familiar place. He opened his eyes, and the back room of Teon's house swam into focus.

He was safe. Relief washed over him as Teon and Reis walked in. Reis was holding a bowl of water and a cloth, and Edgar sat up as they approached, trying to keep his wincing to a minimum. Pain in his ribs betrayed him, and Reis's eyes flashed with concern. They sat at the edge of the bed and slowly raised the hem of his dirty white T-shirt.

"You're not going anywhere." Edgar's heart sank as he heard Reis's words. He knew about his broken ribs—he'd felt them crack underneath Burnell's boots during the interrogation. His fingers hurt so badly he doubted he'd be able to hold a gun, let alone pull the trigger if needed. Yet the idea of staying hidden in Kasyova while Reis fled to Anver was gut-wrenching.

"I'm not letting you go alone," Edgar said. "I refuse to let you go and die on me."

Reis smiled, though the pain and sorrow never left their eyes. "I don't think we have a choice. You can still back me up remotely. You're a hacker anyway—your skills are far more useful if you stay here." They sat on the edge of the bed and dabbed at Edgar's wounds with a warm, wet cloth. Soon the water in the bowl was stained red. Teon took it away to change it, momentarily leaving Edgar and Reis alone.

"This is all my fault," Reis said, their hands in their lap, head bowed, turned away from Edgar. "I should never have let them stroke my ego. What was I thinking, playing at President?"

Edgar reached his hand out and clasped Reis's, trying to ignore the agony in his nail beds. "Reis, we're only human. We did what we could back there. I fully expected to die with you believing I'd betrayed you. That thought hurt more than anything Wynn or Burnell could do to my body." He took a deep breath, fighting with emotions so close to the surface. "I never wanted to hurt Emily. To save you, they made me kill our friend. That's why I want to go with you, Reis. I want revenge. I want to kill every one of those bastards who made me choose between your life and that of a dear friend."

"You can hardly walk. You're in no fit state to travel," Reis said.

"It doesn't matter. We both know we're never coming back."

Reis turned to meet his gaze, their brown eyes wide

as saucers with shock. "Don't say that, Edgar Tobias. We still have so much left to do."

Edgar managed a wan smile, but it flickered and faded. "It might be that people like us weren't made for times of peace. When the chips are down, it's here that we truly come to life. You know as much as I do that we could still walk away from all this, but we won't. The Killing Game changed us. It melted us down and forged us into something new. I was trying to run from that. I blamed you for everything—but the truth is, I want to fight. I need to see Anver prosper again. More than anything, though, I want to say that I didn't just watch from a distance when people needed our help. The Rainbow Bridge was worthwhile, but it was never enough."

"Do you have a plan?" Reis asked.

"I'm working on one. It involves me coming with you." He leaned into Reis's ear and whispered intimately, "I can put Prophet down. I think I've figured everything out, but we have to go soon."

"You're in no fit state to do anything," Reis said. "I insist that we at least get you cleaned up, get some sleep, and have something to eat."

"You might be right," Edgar confessed. "Reis, just promise me you won't leave without me. Swear it."

"I won't," Reis said. "We're in this together until the end."

"Until the end," Edgar promised.

Teon returned with a fresh bowl of water and a large bottle of alcohol, along with a big stack of gauze and bandages. Reis cleaned and wrapped Edgar's wounds;

soon, he was as comfortable as he could get. Reis went to take a shower, leaving Teon alone with him.

"You would go to the ends of the Earth for Reis, wouldn't you?" Teon asked. They perched on the edge of the bed, their hands clasped together in thought.

"More than that," Edgar admitted. "I'd go into the fiery depths of Hell itself for them. I'm coming back, Teon, and I will marry Reis once this is all over."

"You just told Reis that—"

"Reis needs a little motivation. Did you see the look in their eyes? They're different now. They want to live. I just needed to know that before we went back to Anver. I needed to know Reis isn't recklessly throwing their life away, but they're not. They truly believe they can bring Anver's crisis to an end, and so do I."

"Then I wish you luck, kiddo," Teon said. "I'm proud of you. You've grown up to be a fine young man."

"Enough of that," Edgar insisted. "Just give me away at my wedding, and I'll make sure I'm there."

"I wouldn't miss it for the world," Teon said.

Reis returned, clad in a towel. Teon slipped away, closing the door behind them. Reis slid into bed beside Edgar and fell asleep almost immediately. Edgar started to lay out his plan, but the inviting arms of sleep beckoned him in, and he fell into the dark abyss of oblivion before he could form a cohesive thought.

Chapter Thirteen

REIS

Reis rifled through Teon's old wardrobe with a growing sense of exasperation. The suit Reis had worn in their brief stint as President was nice but restricting, and the idea of waltzing into Anver packing heat in a T-shirt and jeans two sizes two big seemed absurd.

"I don't have time to shop for clothes," Reis said. "We're going on the run. I can't worry about my style." They kept their voice down, eyes on the closed door beyond which Edgar was still sleeping.

"Being comfortable in your skin is important, Reis," Teon said. "Especially once you run out of T. Not to mention the importance of ease of movement. Comfort might make the difference between drawing your weapon in time and not."

"Fine. We'll go shopping, but let's make it quick. I don't like the idea of leaving Ed here at the house, and he'll draw too much attention with his injuries." Reis took some of the money and stuffed it into their pocket. Teon grabbed their purse, and they headed out to Teon's car.

They sat in silence most of the way to the mall. Reis looked out the window, their eyes soaking in Kasyova as though they would never see it again. It had become home in a strange sense. It wasn't Anver, yet it was the birthplace of Reis's true self once they'd finally taken the plunge on HRT and surgery. Anver belonged to a different life, a former existence of doubt and reluctance. In many ways, they had no desire to return there, yet the fact that both places felt like home only intensified Reis's desire to bring both cities back together.

Reis splurged on bulletproof vests, tactical pants, and combat boots at the military surplus store as Teon hung back. The leather shop next door had Reis leaving with a trench coat, and they left the pharmacy with several braces and medical supports to help make Edgar's trip a little more comfortable. A computer store yielded a powerful gaming laptop that Reis hoped would be sufficient to run any exploits Edgar needed. He wouldn't be picky about clothing, but Reis had bought him a holster for his pistol regardless and some new clothes that would fit well. It helped to be prepared. Reis felt more positive as they arrived back at Teon's home and dressed in their new outfit. It was similar to what they'd worn back during the Killing Game days, except the face in the mirror had changed, and they could breathe a little easier without a tight binder underneath their shirt.

"Now you look ready to start a revolution," Teon said. Reis nodded. Perhaps it hadn't been so frivolous when they thought about it. It was comforting to know that if the worst came to worst, at least they'd die feeling like themself.

Reis entered the back room and woke Edgar.

"Looking sharp," Edgar said, grinning. "I feel like a sidekick with my T-shirt and jeans. I should have some intense hacker getup or something."

Reis laughed. "Maybe we'll have a neon wedding. Synthpop music and cyberpunk."

"Sounds cool!" Edgar smirked, but it faded as he got up and winced. "Stop fussing." He batted Reis's offer of help aside. "I have to stand on my own two feet. Just tell me you got some painkillers when you went shopping."

Reis nodded. "Had to leave some stuff out of the backpack, but we'll be fine for about a month. We'll have to procure on-site after that."

"Do you believe we can do this, Reis?" Edgar asked.

"I think we have to try. That's all we can do. Maybe we'll get cut to ribbons, but the thought of running to another country and abandoning everyone in need turns my stomach."

"Loyalty to the end," Edgar mused. "Reis, I love you. I don't say it enough, so there you are. Let's get through this."

"Right."

Edgar installed programs on the laptop while Reis showered and dressed. Slipping into the long coat and fastening their holster to their belt felt like coming home. Finally, they were going to take the fight back to Nation Builders. They were going to save Zach, take down Prophet, and end the war.

They traded places. Edgar slipped into the shower room while Reis wandered into the kitchen to grab a bite to eat. Teon stood at the counter, brewing a pot of coffee.

"Might as well enjoy a cup of coffee while you can," Teon explained. "You won't get another one for a while."

Reis nodded. They pulled a rainbow-patterned mug from the cupboard and set it on the counter. Once the pot had stopped dripping, they poured the dark-brown liquid into the cup and added milk and sugar.

"Thanks for everything, Teon. If it wasn't for you, we…" There was no easy way to say what Reis meant. Goodbye was too blunt, despite the sad glimmer in Teon's eyes telling Reis they suspected they wouldn't be coming back.

"You're family, Reis. That's all there is to it. The Soulmates were family, Edgar is family, and so are you." Teon surprised Reis by embracing them in a bear hug. "I know you won't stop fighting until Anver is free but try to think of yourselves. Your lives are valuable to me. If you can't make a difference in Anver, there'll always be a home here for you. I'm not afraid of lying to the authorities if it keeps you safe. So…don't ever feel like you have nowhere to go."

"I'm not going back because I'm being hunted. I'm returning to Anver because the war needs to end. Nation Builders has meddled in Anver's affairs for far too long. The people are suffering from a war I don't believe they want. I have to see for myself, Teon. I have to finish what my father started without his broken intentions."

"Then go with my blessing and good luck to you

both." Teon nodded as Edgar appeared at the kitchen doorway. He gravitated over to the coffee pot, seemingly oblivious that he'd interrupted their discussion.

"Teon, thank you for everything," Edgar said as he poured himself a cup of coffee. "You gave us shelter—but more than that, you've always been there for us."

Teon smiled and hugged Edgar. "You're the son I never had. You make your fathers proud, I know it. You may not have taken a musical path, but you have the same sense of justice flowing through your veins as they did—the intrinsic need to do the right thing. Anver isn't your home country, yet you're returning to fight for its people. That takes courage."

"Thanks," Edgar said. He took a swig of coffee to hide his face, but Reis caught a brief glimmer of tears welling in his eyes. If they didn't get out of there soon, there would be group hugs and tears, and Reis wasn't sure they could bring themself to leave if it came to that. Anver would be a lawless, loveless place, but they needed to go back, or they'd spend the rest of their life wondering if there was something more they could have done.

"We need to go," Reis said, looking at their watch. "I'd like to get in and out of the tunnel under cover of darkness."

Edgar nodded and set their coffee cup down. They met Reis's eyes briefly, and Reis understood that Edgar was having the same problem leaving as they did. It was hard to say goodbye to loved ones and a life that had been mostly kind to them, but Anver called. The city where they'd been forged in blood and fire needed them to come home and save the day one last time.

Teon dropped them off beside the tunnel entrance. Reis watched as their car pulled away into the distance. They drew in a long breath as they took in the lights of a city still alive, and looked across the river to Anver, shrouded in darkness except for a few fires and smoke that drifted upwards and covered the moon.

They let a long breath out as a sigh and walked down the steps to the house that covered the tunnel entrance. Reis lifted the hatch and threw their bag into the tunnel before climbing in. Edgar handed the laptop computer he'd been clutching to his chest to Reis, who carried it down with them. Edgar needed both hands to navigate the ladder with his injuries, but he seemed to hide the worst of his pain.

"Don't look at me like that," Edgar said as he let go of the ladder and took the laptop back from Reis. "I'm not made of glass. I'm not about to break that easily."

"You must be in immense pain…"

"Don't let it distract you, Reis. We came here to complete a task. Let's get it done." Edgar marched forward, leaving Reis trailing behind. Reis scooped up their heavy backpack and followed Edgar down the tunnel.

"So, now that the authorities are not monitoring us, what's the plan?" Reis asked.

"We go in, and we go for Prophet, we take it down. Without the AI spreading propaganda, collecting data, and stoking the flames, Nation Builders will be blind in Anver. They'll have no choice but to pull out. Once they've finished manipulating the situation, the Union

States and the Eastern Federation should realize that continuing their proxy war here is not in their best interests."

"You're forgetting an important variable. One who could sink the entire plan."

"Zach." Edgar sighed. "Reis, I know you care about his fate, but if he's working for them, he's our enemy."

"He's only doing it for his daughter."

"Is he? Can you be sure of that? Even if that's true, what evidence do you have to convince him that she's safe in the hands of the Anver-Kasyova Shadow Government?"

"They wouldn't kill a child," Reis argued.

"They'll do whatever it takes, Reis. That's what they have to do. They can't hold anything sacred. Not you, not me, not even a child. That's why they interrogated me and usurped your position once you were no longer useful to them. They exist to serve the state and nothing else. It's not personal. It's about survival. What happens next will dictate if the Twin City-States survive or are consigned to the history books as another failed state."

"Maybe the Twin City-States should die," Reis said. "If they exist only to hold power at any cost, perhaps Anver-Kasyova should disappear and be replaced by two independent states."

"That's for the people to decide," Edgar said. "Right now, they don't have the power to determine their fate. Truth itself is being manipulated and controlled by Nation Builders, and democracy is in tatters. We have to give the power back to the people. What they decide to do with it is up to them. If the Twin City-States of Anver-Kasyova are no more, I'll abide by that decision. I'm here so that the people can make that choice again."

"Heh…" Reis shifted the backpack on their back and continued walking. "I always thought being a true patriot was about loyalty to an ideal, a vision. I could see the logic in Wynn and Burnell's actions. But a real patriot serves the people, not the idea or identity of a state."

Edgar nodded. "Indeed. That's why we're here. You could have been a good President, Reis."

"I never wanted that kind of power or responsibility. It was a mistake on the part of Wynn and the Shadow Cabinet to think I could fill that role."

"That's why you would have been perfect. The world has been torn apart by people who lust for power and take it by force. Nation Builders has bent truth itself to grab at the reins of power. Maybe we need a President who doesn't aspire to rule. Someone intelligent and strong enough to outwit and destroy the power struggles that demolished the Twin City-States the first time, but honest enough to serve the people's best interests instead of lining their own pockets."

"The former President was a good man."

"Was he? Think about it. If he was so honest, why was Tony Anvas able to gain a foothold? With lies, yes, but for a lie to be believed, it usually must contain some nugget of truth—and that truth is, the former President was in the pockets of Kasyovan lobbyists. He did take money from Anverite science grants and funnel it into Kasyova. It wasn't so hard to take that fact and spin it into a conspiracy theory that Anver existed only to create revenue for Kasyova to flourish. Add to that the fact he seemed to believe he had the rebellious elements of his government under control, and as you can see, it was a recipe for disaster."

They lapsed into silence for a while, Reis chewing over Edgar's words in his mind. Edgar had better grasped the situation. He'd watched and studied while Reis had worked on themself, analyzing the reasons for the fall of the Twin City-States. Reis realized they'd underestimated Edgar far too many times to count. They glanced sideways to notice Edgar wince a little, and a newfound admiration flowed through Reis's veins for their partner—along with guilt that they hadn't recognized so many of Edgar's accomplishments until now.

"Perhaps you should stand for President," Reis offered.

"I prefer the shadows, not the spotlight." Edgar chuckled. "Besides, I don't possess your level of charisma, Reis. I'm fine with being the sidekick."

The end of the tunnel loomed before them, a makeshift ladder leading up to the basement of the suburban home that covered it. They hushed down as Reis first climbed the ladder, pistol in hand, and they opened the trapdoor. It was gloomy, but the immediate vicinity seemed unoccupied, so Reis pushed their backpack through the entrance and climbed up. They turned around, took Edgar's laptop, and helped them through the opening.

Reis felt the unmistakable brush of a gun barrel

against the side of their head and bristled.

"Drop your weapon or die, Kasyovan scum," a husky voice demanded. Reis let the pistol slide from their fingers. It clattered on the floor like a worthless hunk of metal. A shadowy figure crossed in front of them to pick it up. Reis noted from the corner of their eye that a gun was pressed to Edgar's head, too. One false move could mean the end for both of them.

"Put the backpack down—and any other weapons. Hurry up!"

Reis complied. They'd never be able to take out two targets before one fired on Edgar. Better to live now and fight to see another day.

"Move." The gun barrel moved to their back, and Reis stepped forward. They were led outside to a waiting van. Their hands were bound behind their back with rope, and they were hustled into the back. The doors slammed shut, and an engine fired up. With a screech of tires, the van sped away into the night.

Reis caught Edgar's eye, and their same thought was reflected in Edgar's gaze.

This was a mistake.

Chapter Fourteen

EDGAR

Edgar rolled over, his broken rib sending shockwaves of agony through him from having his hands tied behind his back and being thrown down on the hard floor of the van. He tried to keep panic at bay, but this was not a good start to their mission.

But then, what had he expected? Had he anticipated walking into Anver and marching through the ruined streets at dawn unopposed? Had he thought it would be as easy as breaking into Prophet's mainframe and disabling her, end of story? Of course not.

Reis glanced over, and Edgar caught their gaze. He sent what he hoped was a reassuring look and rolled into a sitting position. He gritted his teeth at the pain that flared and took a few deep breaths to keep from passing out. Reis effortlessly sat up, and Edgar envied them for a moment. They would have been better staying in a supporting role back in Kasyova, but no. He could only imagine the fear he would be going through right now to think that Reis was in danger, and he was powerless to save them. He'd decided last time Reis had gone on a mission that he wouldn't let them go alone anymore.

If they died, they died together.

The van pulled up sharply and stopped, interrupting Edgar's gloomy thoughts. The back doors flew open, and Edgar got out of the van voluntarily before he could be roughly dragged out. He was hustled into a dilapidated townhouse in an area that had seen heavy shelling. The distant sound of gunfire reached his ears, and the acrid stench of smoke made his eyes water.

The house was lived in. Newspapers and magazines sat in piles on the living room floor. A young man lay on a torn-up couch, snoring. A middle-aged woman paused when she saw them but then continued as if everything was normal.

Edgar was herded into a basement through a narrow hallway and down narrow stone steps. The basement was bigger than Edgar had imagined and was a hive of activity, with a small army of people typing away on computers and servicing guns. Edgar realized that the walls of every basement in the row of homes had been knocked out to create one huge underground warehouse.

"Keep moving," the man with the gruff voice barked. "She'll be pissed if we're late." Edgar wondered who "she" could pertain to but saw no harm in compliance, at least for now. Reis seemed to agree as they continued behind them until the entourage reached a door set into the far wall. The masked man knocked.

"Come in," a familiar voice said. The door opened

and they were pushed into an office. It was a haven of silence compared to the rest of the basement. An old metal desk sat in the middle of the room, and behind it sat Summer, Leah Mendes's daughter.

Edgar let out a sigh of relief. "Thank fuck. We thought we were going to die. Where have you been? You disappeared as soon as we got to Kasyova."

"Be quiet. Did you scan them?" Summer asked the man, who nodded. "Then leave us alone if you would." The man took the rest of his soldiers and left. He closed the door quietly behind them.

"I apologize for the rough reception," Summer said. "It was necessary." She walked behind Edgar, untied the rope binding his wrists together, then freed Reis. Reis shrugged free from Summer's touch and rubbed their wrists.

"You didn't have to arrest us like criminals," Reis complained. "We came to help free Anver."

"Obviously. You marched in like fresh meat, just waiting to get killed. How naive are you? You'd be dead by now if my men didn't get to you first. That tunnel's been compromised for a while." Summer sighed and gestured to two chairs in front of the desk. "Sit down. We have a lot to talk about."

"We're not interested in joining your little militia," Reis said. "We came here to help the people of Anver, and we can't do that until Prophet is gone and Nation Builders are out of here."

"What do you think I've been trying to do?" Summer asked. "I've been gathering like-minded people together here for a while now. People who are sick of the war and manipulation on social feeds. It's brilliant. Nation Builders has turned information into power. They ensure that a few chosen people can access internet, social media, and television through the Prophet system. These people think they have something special and spread the information they get from the feeds to those who don't have access. They're so happy to be chosen that they don't realize most of it is fake news. As for the television and newspapers—Tony Anvas's network still controls the media. Nation Builders writes the news the way it wants it to be heard. Most Anverites, manipulated and twisted by what they've heard through the grapevine, now openly loathe the Kasyovans. They're one step away from coming together to march on Kasyova, which is Nation Builders' plan. Anver is largely expended now. They want to use the survivors to destroy Kasyova so they can move in on its resources."

"We have to destroy Prophet," Edgar said. "That's the key to all this."

"You say that like the system isn't twenty levels underground, protected by one of the most advanced security systems in the world." Summer shook her head. "There's no getting to Prophet. Short of having someone on the inside, we're fucked."

"Maybe we do have someone on the inside," Reis said.

"We have no way of contacting Zach," Edgar said. "Even if we could, there's no guarantee he'd help us."

"You could do it," Reis replied. "You're a hacker. Isn't

there some way you can leave him a message through Prophet?"

"Even if I could get into the system, what kind of message could I leave that Prophet wouldn't figure out? Even if I could get a message through, and even if Zach agrees to help, how could he do it? His hands are tied. He's as good as Prophet's prisoner since he went inside the Pyramid."

"You're talking about that failed black op?" Summer asked. "That was Kasyova?"

"Yeah." Edgar kept quiet about the Shadow Government. They might have pulled out his fingernails, but he wasn't about to break his oath and disclose their existence, even if Nation Builders already knew.

Reis, however, didn't share the same compunctions. "No. Not Kasyova. The Twin City-States Shadow Government. They operate beneath Kasyova, trying to save the union."

"They didn't do a very good job of it," Summer remarked. "The op was a total failure. The Union States blamed the Eastern Federation for it, and fighting flared up in the aftermath."

"They had an AI system like Prophet, called Oracle," Edgar disclosed. "She was compromised. Nation Builders knew everything that the Shadow Government was planning." He closed his eyes, regret running through his veins. "I stopped her, but it was too late. Nation Builders knows everything. That's why we came alone. To end Prophet ourselves and get Nation Builders, the Union States, and the Eastern Federation out of here."

"We've been working on trying to counter Prophet's fake news network," Summer said. "The most we've been able to manage are radio broadcasts, but they've brought a surprising number of recruits in. People know things aren't adding up, and once they hear the truth, they can recognize that they've been fed nothing but lies."

Reis nodded. "People want Anver-Kasyova back?"

"They never wanted it to end. It took a lot of bad actors to destabilize a stable regime after ten years of peace. Sure, Anvas's false promises sucked in some, yet all but the most diehard have realized Anvas was a traitor to his country and democracy. The extremists have received a lot of funding, soldiers, and weapons from the Union States and the Eastern Federation to keep fighting. Public opinion, swayed by the Anvas Media Group worldwide, has kept them in the war. Foreigners believe that this war is about independence."

"Then we have to show them otherwise," Edgar said. "What can we do to help, Summer?"

Reis looked over at him, but Edgar glanced down at the bandaged hands in his lap. "Our plan wasn't a great one, Reis. Marching into the Pyramid expecting to take down Prophet...it was a suicidal last-ditch effort. We have options now. We can stay and help build the Resistance here and stand a fighting chance of freeing Anver from the grip of Nation Builders."

"He's a smart one," Summer said. "You should listen to him, Reis. Throwing your lives away on a mission doomed to fail will set us back months. We need your help, both now and in the aftermath of the war. The truth is, I knew about the Shadow Government. We were in contact with them until recently when all communications went silent. I know they chose you to be their President—and that you cast it aside to come here and help the people. It must be frustrating to be stuck serving an organization again, but you can't hope to defeat Nation Builders alone. Nor should you. One person having all that power got us into this mess in the first place. We let Tony Anvas buy up every media corporation in Anver until he was the only face on our television screens. Until he owned every fiber-optic cable beneath the city, every Internet connection, every video service, so he could twist the Killing Game story however he wanted to."

Reis fell silent. Edgar could only hope Summer's words had struck a chord in them—and it seemed like they had.

"Anyway, you must be tired," Summer said. "It's no luxury hotel, but I'll have my people find you a quiet, comfortable room upstairs so you can sleep."

"Thank you," Edgar said. As Resistance soldiers entered and led them upstairs, Reis never turned to look at Edgar even once. Edgar thought about saying something, but exhaustion pulled at him. It had been a long day, his rib hurt, his fingers stung, and any conversation would likely turn into an argument. Better they made plans after they woke up when they had fresh minds to pick over their change of plans.

The soldier who led them into the bedroom wore a red handkerchief over their face and kept their assault rifle at the ready. It was a reminder that they weren't safe here, that their reprieve might not last long. The room had bare floorboards with two well-used sleeping bags in the middle. Moth-eaten curtains hung limply over the window, stray moonlight seeping through the holes. Still, to Edgar, it looked like a palace. Here, they could buy time and think things through.

Maybe they stood a chance after all.

Chapter Fifteen

REIS

Reis waited until Edgar's breathing slowed and evened out. A light snore told Reis that he was out, and they sat up. They moved the sleeping bag gently and fumbled for their clothes, acutely aware that one creaking floorboard could disturb Edgar and throw their entire plan into jeopardy.

They weren't going to wait on an organization again. Reis had let the Shadow Government call too many shots until they felt they'd lost ownership of themself. The Resistance would use and discard them the same way, and Reis was done with being used. Done with waiting for others to act. Done with taking orders like a cog in someone else's machine.

It was time to make a difference in the best way they knew how: with direct action.

Reis looked down at Edgar's face. He looked so serene in sleep, though the bruises and marks on his face marred the illusion of peace. Edgar had suffered enough, and that was another reason to go alone. Edgar had no desire to lose his life in a suicide mission—but Reis had made their peace with it long ago. Edgar had been right about one thing—peace was not for them. Their father had trained and bred Reis to be a warrior—a child soldier—and now they were an adult, nothing but the adrenaline rush of fighting and fucking held any meaning. Even the moment of peace after escaping Anver the last time had left them feeling like a cat on hot bricks, dancing about restlessly, waiting for the moment to come when they would strike back.

This was their true self as much as any physical characteristics. They'd come to accept it slowly. It had been harder to come to terms with than the truth of being trans when they thought about it. To be nonbinary was accepted and largely understood in the modern world. To be a natural-born killer, however, still marked one as a pariah amongst people, a human who had scratched away the veneer of humanity to embrace the animal beneath.

Edgar had never really believed that person existed. He'd always argued for the fact that Reis had protected him during the Killing Game as proof of their humanity. Reis had wanted to be the person Edgar saw so badly, but it just wasn't to be.

Reis tiptoed out of the room without looking back. They picked up their weapons and enough rations from the storage room next door for a few days. They felt complete again with a weapon at their side.

It was time to end this. To end Anver's pain and

suffering once and for all. Prophet—and those who would defend it—had to die. The Resistance and the Shadow Government, along with Edgar, could fight the long war for hearts and minds in the aftermath, but nothing would change unless someone took drastic action and made the first move. Reis was done with waiting to die. They embraced the end if it meant they could finally achieve some purpose in this life. If they could use the skills their father had taught them and put a bullet in those who would seek to undermine Anver's future, it would all be worth it.

Three soldiers sat on a ratty couch in the living room, watching Anvas's media network pump out propaganda on a battery-powered tablet screen. Reis tiptoed past the entrance and down the hallway to a side door that led out into an alley. They waded through the mountain of trash and discarded needles that had built up since public services had ended. The back alleys of Anver smelled like death, and Reis was unsurprised to see rats as big as cats scurrying about, along with mangy dogs and starved cats. Reis pitied the pets who had been left to fend for themselves but knew they'd be mauled by a pack of dogs if they offered a portion of their rations to the hungry animals. They forced themself to move on through the dark alleyways toward the city center.

A dead body lay face down in the gutter. Reis drew their pistol and looked about for any signs they were being watched, but the night was surprisingly quiet. On closer inspection, Reis realized the woman's throat had been slit days ago. They fought back bile and pressed on, keeping in the shadows even when few seemed to be found.

Downtown, once the home of majestic historical buildings standing alongside modern architectural marvels, was nothing more than abstract piles of rubble and steel. The glass buildings Anver was known for stood like skeletons in the moonlight, their windows shattered, leaving only the framework to prove they'd ever been there.

Anver's Hospital Tower still glowed in the night—an ominous red, the same color since the crisis began. Some of the rings no longer functioned, but even the Union States and the Eastern Federation had been careful to avoid targeting the hospital. It was a case of bad optics that even the Anvas Media Group couldn't hide if the lights went out forever.

Reis was glad for a landmark in a city that seemed alien to them now. Once they'd known every street, every alley, but now the city was incomprehensible, streets carved around ruins. Still, the occasional flash of headlights could be seen, the few privileged enough to continue pretending at a normal life coming and going through the war-torn city. Reis wondered what it must be like to live like that, in constant denial of Anver's destruction while it stared them in the face.

Gunfire rang out close to their position, and Reis ducked behind a wall. City Hall still stood, the classical building damaged but not down. They climbed the steps and skirted around the building. Floodlights shone out front, and Reis spied rebel soldiers marching around prisoners kneeling on the plaza. They thought about enacting a rescue, but their eyes strayed to the broken pyramid at Government Hill. They didn't have time to get caught up in a hopeless battle here when their final destination was so close.

They closed their eyes as they walked away, and shots rang out behind them. Edgar wouldn't have walked away. He would have devised a way to save them, even if it jeopardized the mission. That was the kind of guy he was. The kind of guy Reis loved, deep down, even if they weren't sure that Edgar would love them if he could see this side of them. The ruthless side. They'd argued about it before Emily's wedding, separating for a while because of it. Reis had put it down to distancing themselves from their feelings because of their dysphoria, but T hadn't been the game-changer they'd hoped in that regard. Certainly, their dysphoria had lessened, and there were times they felt euphoria instead, but the craving for action and adrenaline had never ceased. The desire to fight to the bitter end for something, to feel like they mattered in a world where people's efforts seemed to mean less and less each day.

Government Hill was a slog. The roads that had once been impeccably kept lay in ruins, bombed out by airstrikes early in the crisis. High-security fences, barbed wire, and turrets surrounded the once-welcoming building that had been the seat of government. Drones buzzed about like bees. Reis lay in the overgrown bushes, trying to formulate a plan, when a drone flew over and took a picture with an audible snap. They raised their pistol and shot it out of the sky. The drone crashed to the ground in a shower of sparks, causing a small fire.

"You don't need to hide, Reis Asher. I've been expecting you." A familiar voice boomed from the building, cast loud and wide by the PA system that had once summoned senators to sessions. The front gates opened automatically, the large steel barriers sliding back.

Reis knew it was almost certainly a trap, but any attempt at stealth was pointless now. Prophet knew they were here. Either they went forward hoping to construct a plan on the way, or they fled with their tail tucked between their legs.

They weren't turning back now. Not after everything they'd come through to get here. The Killing Game. The thousand times they'd almost lost Edgar. Losing Emily Vos—twice. The betrayal of their father and all they'd held dear. To turn away now would be spitting in the face of everyone who had sacrificed themselves to get Reis to this point.

Reis stepped forward. The bodies of the team the Shadow Government had sent in still rotted in the front gardens, scattered across the walkways like broken dolls. Their blood had turned brown. Reis felt regretful, but it hadn't been their plan. They'd just done whatever Burnell and Wynn had asked of them, rubber-stamping the mission with the hope that both knew what they were doing. They'd been a bad President, and they knew it.

Reis walked to the main entrance. The double doors opened automatically. Lights turned on as they stepped into the marble entranceway. A statue of their father in bronze stood tall in the vestibule, a quill in his hand. "The Father of Unification," the plaque read. Reis closed their eyes momentarily. Even after he'd been discredited, he'd still been held up as a misguided hero, used and abused by greater powers. Perhaps that was the truth. Maybe he and Reis weren't so different after all. Reis wanted to believe that their father had believed in Unification, but hearing the truth from his mouth had tarnished the sheen of his legacy.

Before that, they'd been able to justify everything in a twisted sense. Being a child soldier hadn't seemed so unforgivable when a hero trained them to shoot. When Reis had been defending the country by putting a bullet in a would-be assassin's head. However, it had all been designed to fail. Designed to crumble and fall apart and plunge Anver into war again, and that made every wrong stand out. Elias Torell had trained his child to be a soldier to carry out his will and wishes, depriving them of a normal life. Reis would never be able to sit quietly in a career and spend lazy Sunday mornings reading the newspaper. A piece of them would always crave the moment on the edge of death, the high-stakes zero-sum game that was war.

"You've arrived." Reis jumped out of their skin and pointed their pistol at the figure who emerged from the shadows. Zach stood beside the statue of Reis's father, looking tired and haggard. "He sent me to greet you, Reis. I suppose you're the guest of honor today."

"What does that mean?" Reis asked. "Whose guest?"

"Lower the gun, Reis. You won't shoot me. Just

hurry up already. He's getting impatient."

"Prophet?" Reis holstered their gun. Zach was right—Reis had no intention of shooting him. They shrugged and followed Zach into a large elevator at the back of the vestibule. Zach scanned the ID badge he was wearing around his neck against a pad on the elevator wall, and it began to plunge downward. Reis looked into the corner to see a gun turret trained on them and swallowed, their throat suddenly dry. They were safe—so long as they were a valued guest. Once they ceased to be useful to their host, or if they showed any signs of resistance, the automated defenses would take care of them faster than they could count to three.

"Your daughter is safe, Zach. You don't have to do this anymore. We found the bomb and removed it. She's going to be okay—"

"I know." Zach shrugged. "Did you expect me to flip sides, knowing that?"

"I just thought you'd want to know," Reis replied.

"Okay, then," Zach said. The elevator ground to a halt, and the doors slid open. Zach led Reis down a long hallway and opened a door. He led Reis into a room that was the same as the situation room in the Shadow Government's base of operations. Monitors lined the walls, lit up with various shots of Anver in states of decay.

A figure cast in shadow sat in a chair studying the monitors. The chair spun to reveal Tony Anvas, dressed in a crisp black suit, black hair freshly dyed, and not looking a day over fifty. Zach left Reis's side and went to stand beside Tony. Of course, Reis realized, they were lovers, after all. In the final stages of their plan, Zach was the last one who stood beside Anvas.

"The country's assembling against you, and the rest of the world is losing interest in the war," Reis said. "It's over, Anvas. Shut down Prophet and leave Anver for good."

Anvas chuckled. "I can't believe you don't get it, Reis Asher. Why I'm here. Why Nation Builders is here. Why I started the Killing Game in the first place."

"I can't say I do," Reis admitted. "It's never been about Anver's independence; I know that much."

"It was, once," Anvas admitted. "When I ran with your father, we were young and idealistic. Nation Builders didn't even exist, then. We wanted Anver to prosper and were willing to give anything to see that happen."

"You built Unification with a caveat," Reis said. "You never believed in the Twin City-States. You only accepted it as a compromise. You set up the Killing Game to destabilize Unification. At some point between then and now, the original minds behind Unification came together to form the Killing Committee, also known as Nation Builders, to manipulate Anver's image to the rest of the world and start an international proxy war so you could grab power and profit while destabilizing the two world superpowers. That much I understand. What I don't get is why you're still here. What does turning Anver to rubble do for you and your ideology? Why did so many have to die, and what is your endgame?"

Anvas huffed. "First off, the Killing Committee and Nation Builders are different, though I can see how a layperson might become confused. When your father, I, and others sought to change Anver's fate, we created the Committee to plan the Killing Game and the eventual undoing of Unification. After Unification, though, your father and I were approached and offered a very special privilege—membership in the organization known as Nation Builders. It was as though the doors to a secret world opened up to us when the peace treaty was signed. Nation Builders is an organization of the greatest minds the world has ever seen, Reis. They paint the broad strokes of the canvas of world politics and seek to put the world on a better path so that humanity doesn't destroy itself."

"If that's true, why is Anver in ruins? Nation Builders has twisted the truth and turned the Twin Cities against one another! They've used Anver's greatest invention— the true AI in Oracle and Prophet—as a weapon to gas- light the people into a war they don't want!"

"We had no choice." Anvas sighed. "Anver-Kasyova was too brilliant for its own good. Our greatest minds warned that AI would spell the end of the human race— and here we had two AIs, built in secret, that contained enough brainpower to destroy the world. We had to ruin Anver, don't you see? We had to destroy that knowledge before it could become part of the mainstream."

"You had to turn the lives of Anverites upside down for that? You couldn't simply send in agents to destroy the research?"

"We've been fighting to keep the AIs contained here. Edgar Tobias did us a huge favor by taking Oracle out of the picture. That leaves Prophet."

"So shut it down!" Reis yelled.

"It's not that simple!" Zach interjected. "Do you think Nation Builders would destroy a country if Prophet could be shut down?"

"Edgar managed to eliminate Oracle. Do the same here. It's just a computer, for fuck's sake."

Anvas got up and started to pace the room. "I loved your father, Reis. After his wife—your mother—was killed, we started seeing each other. I think he was ashamed of me. He never told you about us, did he?"

Zach flinched a little.

"You're lying!" Reis yelled.

"Reis, there are things you don't understand and wouldn't believe if I told you. Yes, your father and I were in love. Believe it or not, it's true. We were young patriots and wanted our home to be the best. We wanted it to be free. We wanted it to go back to being the utopia it started as. Before any of the civil wars that Prophet started."

Reis blinked. "Wait, what? I thought Prophet was a recent creation?"

"Far from it. The Prophet Project started at the end of the last century. We've always wanted to be gods, Reis, and the only way to be a god is to create a new life form. We've been working toward that goal since we walked upright." Anvas swallowed. "What do you know from the history books about Anver and Kasyova's founding stories?"

"We broke off from the Eastern Federation, forming Anver and Kasyova out of the greatest cities of the Federation," Reis offered.

"Wrong. Where Anver and Kasyova stood was a wasteland, a forgotten corner of the Eastern Federation that had been stripped of its natural resources and discarded. Some idealists decided they wanted to build the cities of the future—utopian city-states where war would be nothing but a memory. The goal of these cities would be to advance science and the arts. So they created Anver for science and Kasyova to focus on the arts, each with an AI to govern it. Of course, the technology at the time was crude and human beings were still needed to oversee the daily running of the cities...but that changed. Soon, with the advent of real neural networks, the AIs became self-aware and started to run the cities themselves. The senators only existed to give the cities a veneer of respectability in a world that expects democracy to be the cornerstone of any civilized society. That would be fine, but...the AIs started to veer off the path set for them by their creators. It was Prophet who lit the spark of the first Anver Civil War, Reis."

"Even if this crazy story is true...why? Why would an AI designed to run the city turn its people against one another?" Reis asked.

"Human beings stagnate in a time of peace, that's why," Zach explained. "Prophet felt that Anver's best years were behind it, that its growth rate had slowed significantly. To further its goal of scientific advancement, it decided to give Anver a little motivation in the form of war. Nothing starts an arms race like fighting."

"Elias and I were blind to all of this," Anvas explained. "We truly believed we were fighting in a real war.

I was in awe when Elias told me he had a moment of inspiration and pitched Unification to me. It was such a simple yet elegant solution. I wondered why he wanted safeguards, but I was too smitten with him to ask questions, so I took his claim that he feared for Anver's identity and independence long-term at face value. I didn't know about Prophet or Oracle until Nation Builders approached us. Elias had figured it out, but I had no idea."

"So what?" Reis shook their head. "So, the Twin City-States are ruled by artificial intelligence. Other than the obvious lack of democracy, what's the problem?"

"Prophet has stockpiled nukes," Zach explained. "She truly believes that Anver's way of life is superior to any other on Earth. Oracle kept her at bay, but Prophet has become unhinged now that she's gone. She's ready to destroy the world in a global nuclear war."

"You still haven't explained why we can't just shut the system down. Oracle is gone—why can't we stop Prophet and embrace democracy?"

"Oracle was always the more stable of the two AI systems," Zach continued. "Oracle was welcoming and open—Prophet, by comparison, is paranoid. We can't access her system because her core isn't here. She moved it."

"Then where is it?" Reis asked.

"Inside the people of Anver," Anvas said, spreading his arms wide as if he'd been waiting for Reis to ask the question. "DNA has an incredibly high storage density. Using synthetic DNA strands and a set of enzymes, she used your bodies for biochemical computing."

"How is that possible?" Reis asked, acutely aware that this was something far beyond their understanding. It would be easy for Anvas to use them by talking over their head, inventing justifications for the war that were little more than fiction. "Wouldn't something like that require widespread medical intervention?"

"Everyone has compulsory military service, do they not? Do you remember those so-called antibiotic patches you had to wear during basic training? There's your delivery vector, the subdermal implantation of biocomputing components that made your bodies store and compute data for her. She recreated herself as a decentralized network that cannot be destroyed unless almost every able-bodied adult Anver citizen is killed."

Reis wondered if Anvas's crazy talk could possibly be true. "Is that why you killed so many people? To weaken her network?" It made sense. Too much sense. The best lies held a nugget of truth, but this didn't feel like a lie. There was something like admiration in Anvas's voice. Reis had the sinking feeling that they were in way over their head, seeking simple solutions to incredibly complex problems.

"Nation Builders has to act, Reis, or the world will be destroyed. This proxy war was the best way, so we manipulated the truth using Prophet—or rather, all of you. We fed you false information and twisted the narrative to confuse her. To set her network against itself. To start a war that would thin Anver's population enough that shutting down her secondary systems would render her dormant."

"We're people, Anvas! What you've done is murder!" Reis yelled. They felt like a child stating the obvious, but sometimes ambiguity needed to be cut with a knife.

Anvas looked like a mad man, a feverish passion burning in his eyes, and Reis realized he was no scalpel. They were both blunt instruments for their respective sides. "Indeed, and our Creator will judge me at the end of my life like everyone else. But I did it for the world, Reis Asher. I did it because, left unchecked, the human race will perish!"

Reis held their finger on the trigger. They had a clear shot, and one was all it would take.

"Go ahead. I've wanted to die for a long time. Becoming part of Nation Builders and seeing the truth of the world—how fragile we all are—has destroyed me. Elias told me to take care of you if he could no longer. For the longest time, I thought he wanted me to initiate you into Nation Builders. I had Ash call you and get you involved in the Killing Game to test your worthiness. Now I realize he wanted you to stay as far away from all this as possible. Away from Nation Builders. Away from the truth of the world—because ignorance truly is bliss."

Chapter Sixteen

EDGAR

Edgar woke to a stream of sunlight pouring in through the moth-eaten curtains. He stretched out and opened his eyes, surprised to see Reis's bedroll empty. He'd been the early riser for years, always up first thing in the morning to enjoy coffee and coding before breakfast. Today of all days was a strange day to sleep in—but his body was healing from the after-effects of torture, so he didn't think too deeply about it.

Until Summer came storming into the decrepit bedroom with a frown on her face. "Have you seen Reis lately?"

"No," Edgar admitted. "I just woke up."

"They're not anywhere on the base, and a scout returned this morning to say there was a small fire on Government Hill. Someone downed a drone up there, but they couldn't get close enough to determine whether it was an accident or an attack."

"Fuck." Edgar pushed the sleeping bag off him and

reached for his pants. Reis's clothes were gone, and, judging from the look of their backpack, they'd taken a few things with them. Their weapons were gone as well. Not that Edgar believed they'd gone for a midnight stroll, but the sinking feeling in his gut confirmed his worst fears: Reis had gone after Prophet alone.

"What are you planning?" Summer asked. "You can't go after them. Nobody gets anywhere near Government Hill. Automatic defenses surround the Pyramid."

"I won't just give Reis up for dead!" Edgar yelled. "We came here to do this together, and I'm not backing out now."

"So, what—you're just going to stroll up to Government Hill and get gunned down by turrets to prove a point?"

"No. Look, Reis is reckless, but they're not stupid. They wouldn't just march through gunfire without a plan. They may still be up there waiting for help. If they are, I can't just leave them." Edgar grabbed his pistol and buckled the holster over his jeans. "You don't have to help me, Summer. You have your battles to fight, and I respect that and everything else you're doing here. I want you to keep fighting the good fight, but this is personal for me. Reis is...Reis is the love of my life. Everybody thinks I'm with them because I feel beholden to them for saving my life during the Killing Game, but it was never like that. Reis...Reis makes me feel like I'm somebody. Like I matter. This flesh-and-bones failure of a celebrity child, average coder, and shitty script kiddie hacker can move mountains with them around."

"That's why you thought they should be President," Summer observed.

"I still believe that. I want Reis to stand again if the Twin City-States gets through this crisis. I think it's the only role that will satisfy them because Reis was born to change the world and can't be satisfied with mediocrity like the rest of us." Edgar grabbed his laptop bag and slung it over his shoulder. He winced as his broken rib protested at its weight. "I'd walk through fire for them, and someday, the rest of the Twin City-States will feel the same way I do."

"Well, you might just get that chance," Summer said. "Reis came here to die, Edgar. Are you willing to take a bullet for them?"

"Yes," Edgar said without hesitation.

"Then I wish you luck," Summer said. "I'll have one of my scouts lead you as close to Government Hill as they can safely manage. The rest is on you, Ed."

"Thank you," Edgar said.

*

Edgar gripped his pistol as the small car sped through the crumbling city streets. His eyes widened at the destruction he witnessed, and he swallowed down the guilt that flooded to the surface as he battled with the thought that he and Reis had left everyone for dead when they'd fled to Kasyova. What disturbed him so much was how quiet the city seemed, despite the sounds of gunfire in the distance. Where had all the citizens gone? Had they flooded across the border into neighboring countries, or were they all dead?

"Most of them are underground," the scout said. "Anverites are a hardy lot. We've done this before. Most people still have their shelters and hiding places from the last war. If you went into the subway, you'd see a hive of activity. Anver isn't dead yet."

"Good." Edgar remembered the place he'd come to call home with nostalgia. It was hard to see the bright, modern city he'd known in the piles of rubble and shattered glass that filled the downtown area. The landmarks and character of the city had been flattened, but as long as the people still survived, they would rebuild. Anver would rise again to be twice as beautiful as before.

The car pulled up beside a broken sidewalk, and the scout engaged the parking brake. "This is where we part ways," he said with a shrug. "Too many drones up ahead. I can't risk it. You'll have to climb Government Hill by yourself."

"Thank you," said Edgar. "No need to apologize. I can take it from here." With a deep breath, he opened the car door and got out. He closed the door as softly as he could. He hunkered in some nearby shrubbery until the scout pulled away, and the sounds of the car's engine faded from view. He was scared, his hands trembling slightly, but he rebalanced the strap of his laptop case on his shoulder and held his pistol at the ready. It was now or never, and the longer he hesitated, the more trouble Reis was likely getting themself into.

He was a little stung that Reis had decided to go

alone. Weren't they partners in this? They'd come from the Killing Game together, surviving whatever the world threw at them. They'd returned to Anver to settle this thing as equals, but Edgar felt like the sidekick left at home for his own good. Hadn't he earned his place at Reis's side time and time again with his intelligence, resourcefulness—and, when it came down to it—by neutralizing those who would have killed Reis?

He marched up the hill, trying to push his depressing thoughts away. He told himself that Reis was trying to keep him safe because they loved him. Reis wanted Edgar to survive no matter what. But it still hurt. He hurt because he'd endured torture to save Reis, yet it still felt like he wasn't good enough to accompany them on their little adventure into the heart of madness.

Focus, he reminded himself. Government Hill was overgrown, which largely protected him from the drones' view, but now and then, he was forced to squat in a bush or back up against a tree to avoid detection. It only grew more difficult as he came close to the shattered Glass Pyramid, the former seat of government. The barbed wire fence surrounding the compound was compromised in a dozen places, and it wasn't hard for Edgar to crawl through—though the other side was a different matter. Security cameras scanned almost every inch of the compound, and there were no shadows in the harsh midday light with the sun directly overhead.

He thought about revealing himself but was reminded of the team the Shadow Government had sent in when he spied a human-shaped form on the ground. The blood had faded to a dirty brown, but flies swarmed the corpse, making Edgar queasy as he imagined the rotting flesh underneath. He'd be the same if he announced himself. Instead, he backed himself out through the wire fence and found a well-shaded spot beneath a large tree with several bushes at the foot of it. He pulled out his laptop and booted it up, hyperaware that a drone could hear the laptop fans and come speeding over at any moment, but it never happened. His fingers sped over the keyboard as he connected to the Pyramid's still-operational Wi-Fi network with a password crack he was sure was out of date.

Luck was on his side, but hadn't he always been lucky? The Killing Game had taken a dozen victims before him, and none had found a guardian angel like Reis. Everything he did now, he did because he'd been lucky enough to meet Reis Asher. Fortunate enough to fall in love with them. If his luck ran out today, it was okay. He wouldn't have come this far if it wasn't for fortune smiling on him. Hopefully, it would hold out a little longer so he could save Reis.

He cleared his mind and focused on the task in front of him. The Pyramid's security system was no laughing matter. Edgar wasn't even sure if he was finding a backdoor into Prophet or if the building had a separate system, but it seemed to take forever to make his way in and even longer to shut down the cameras, unlock the doors, and send the drones to investigate the other side of the building for suspicious activity. He snapped the laptop lid closed and let out the breath he'd been holding for a solid minute as the drone closing on his location buzzed further and further away.

He knew it had been all too easy as he approached the main building. It had been a long shot coming here at all. If he'd been turned away empty-handed, he wouldn't have been that surprised, but something had told him to come anyway, that he'd forever regret it if he didn't make an effort. Even if it was a trap with Reis caught in Prophet's web, he didn't want them to die alone. They'd started this thing together and were going to end it together.

Edgar walked through the double doors into a surprisingly intact vestibule. The bombs that had destroyed the building's glass "pyramid" fascia hadn't penetrated the fortified internal structure. Reis's father, Elias Torell, stared at him from a statue cast in bronze. There had been a campaign to take the statue of the discredited figure down, but Anverites were proud of their history, and the statue of one of Anver's most divisive figures remained standing at the seat of government. It held out an olive branch, but its blank eyes made it seem like Torell was about to snatch it back at any moment. Or perhaps that was just Edgar's imagination in light of all that had happened.

The elevator in the back of the room caught his eye. He raised his pistol as the doors opened, but the car was empty. The light inside flickered, beckoning him in.

So, the hack hadn't been a hack. Prophet had let him in while testing his capabilities as a hacker. Despite his desire to run away, he knew that Reis awaited him somewhere below. Perhaps Prophet had allowed them in, too, luring them to their death. Maybe stepping into that elevator was the last thing Edgar would do, but, looking around, there weren't many other options. They'd wasted enough time trying to get into the building, and clearly, Prophet knew he was here, so the idea of trying to sneak down the stairwell seemed ill-conceived at best.

Edgar crossed the marble floor, walking over the seal of the Twin City-States. Once upon a time, the senators and the President convened here, talking over policy in the chamber while beneath them, a plot to overthrow the government was coming together, started by malcontents and instigated by the Killing Committee, bankrolled by Nation Builders. He wished he could go back in time and snuff out the candle of insurrection before it could grow into a fire, but old Anver-Kasyova was gone. If the Twin City-States survived this, it would be with a new Anver who could stand as Kasyova's equal, not with Anver as the sidekick to Kasyova's main event.

Edgar stood with his hands on the trigger of his lowered pistol, ready to raise it at any sign of trouble. The elevator lurched, then sped down so fast that Edgar was convinced it wouldn't stop, that Prophet was trying to kill him. His last meal threatened to leave his body, and he fought back Ashe rising bile in his throat as the elevator started to slow, then stopped. The doors opened with a gentle chime, causing Edgar to let out a *humph* of derision as he stepped out of the elevator into a dimly lit corridor. There was nowhere to go but forward, toward the double doors in front of him, so he went, keeping his legs apart and his pistol ready in case he had to shoot at short notice.

The doors slid back to reveal a huge antechamber. Monitors covered the walls, showing scenes from around Anver. Dwarfed in the middle of the room before several large banks of consoles stood Zach, Tony Anvas, and Reis.

"Edgar! What are you doing here?" Reis asked.

"Did you think I would just let you leave me behind again? Reis, we're in this together. Since you saved my life during the Killing Game, this has been our battle. I refuse to sit by while you march to your death."

Zach glanced down at his shoes. Anvas laughed. "The more, the merrier," he said. "I suppose I should catch you up on what I told Reis here. These consoles run my media network, Edgar, but they're nothing more than Prophet's feelers. The source code for Prophet is inside all of you, implanted as synthetic DNA strands when you entered military service. You did your military service in Anver, isn't that right, Edgar? You wanted to be as close to the city you loved as possible. Well, you got a little more than you bargained for. How does it feel to know an AI hijacked your body to store some of its code? That you're nothing more than a piece of a network, a biochemical computer?"

"That's not all of it," Reis countered. "Oracle and Prophet were designed to rule the cities. The democracy of the Twin City-States—it's a lie. The Twin City-States was designed to be a utopia run by AI, buried beneath the facade of a democratically elected government. The elections, the senators, even the President were all chosen by Prophet and Oracle to further the cities' stated goals—Kasyova to advance the arts, and Anver to research science and technology."

Edgar's heart sank. "Are you saying I destroyed the heart of Kasyova? But—but why? And how? Oracle asked me to implant the virus into her. She told me that Reis would be killed if I didn't."

"Oracle was less advanced than Prophet," Anvas explained. "Her network was stored beneath Kasyova, and you killed her. You freed Kasyova, Edgar—but that drove Prophet over the edge. She's readying Anver's nuclear stockpile as we speak. She'll destroy the world in her madness. This is the very thing that Nation Builders set out to prevent. The whole reason we provoked the war was to destroy the AIs and free the Twin City-States from AI control."

Edgar shook his head. "We were doing just fine without your help, Anvas. The way I see it, if there's anyone to blame for this, it's Nation Builders. Nobody asked you to intervene in our destiny. The residents of Anver were happy until you controlled the news and told them why they shouldn't be. Until you sent assassins to kill innocent people for money." Edgar leaned on a console, trying to stop his head from spinning. His gut churned with horror at the thought that he'd destroyed Oracle without knowing what she truly was. There was no way the Twin City-States could return to what they were—and it was all because of him.

"You were happy living in a dictatorship?" Anvas's

voice was strained with incredulity. "Happy to be puppets in a system where a computer chose your representatives?"

"That's the problem with people like you," Edgar argued. "You always think you know what's best for everyone else. That your way is the right way to live. The Twin City-States prospered, Anvas. Kasyova was number one in the world for creative and artistic output and Anver was number one in scientific and medical development until the war. The first Anverite civil war—were you pulling the strings behind the curtain then, too?"

"I didn't know about any of this back then. It was only when Unification was about to become final that Nation Builders approached me and told me the truth about the country I'd been living in. That's why I got Elias to agree to an exit strategy. I knew I'd be back to free my home, but at the time, we needed peace."

"So, Nation Builders already existed before the war?" Reis chimed in.

"Yes. I don't know if they started the first civil war. It's irrelevant. What matters is that AI cannot be allowed to dominate and destroy the world—and that's precisely what will happen if Prophet is allowed to continue unchecked."

"What's your plan?" Edgar asked. "Destroy Prophet, I suppose. Purge the network from every person in Anver, even if that means killing them. What then? Install a government of your choosing? That's the problem with modern democracy. There is no such thing anymore, even if the system was entered into in good faith. The power elites choose or become the representatives of the people. The wealthy get to dominate the poor. The majority gets to decide for the minority. People like you—people who think you know what's best for everyone else—get to call the shots based on the world you want to see. A world that serves you and your interests alone." Edgar pulled out his laptop and set it up on the console. "You say Prophet is mad, but has anyone thought of trying to prove that theory? From where I'm standing, Anvas, all I see is someone trying to protect their home and their life from a foreign invader—you and Nation Builders."

"What are you going to do?" Anvas asked. "You're going to talk to Prophet and ask it very nicely to please put the nukes away?" Anvas stepped toward Edgar, but Reis raised their pistol, and Anvas stopped. "You, too, Reis? Have you lost your mind?"

"I haven't made up my mind yet, but I want to see the truth with my own eyes," Reis said. "Let Edgar do what he needs to."

"Zach, do something!" Anvas barked. "This is the future of our world we're talking about! We can't let AI get a stranglehold on government, or soon the entire world will be ruled by machines!"

"Maybe that's for the best." Zach shrugged. "Us humans haven't done a very good job of it, have we? Look at the Union States and the Eastern Federation. Locked in a petty pissing contest over who has the best philosophy. Maybe it's time for someone more logical to take control—someone who can balance the needs of everyone in their care."

"You would turn away from me after everything we've been through?" The hurt in Anvas's eyes looked genuine enough to Edgar as he took the briefest glance out of the corner of one eye, which was somehow satisfying. He connected the computer back into the network, hoping to contact Prophet like he'd contacted Oracle.

"You don't need to bother with that, Edgar. I know who you are." They all turned around, shocked as Prophet's voice boomed through the facility. Reis kept their pistol trained on Anvas, but their attention strayed momentarily to the red-hued ghost standing before them. "You killed my sister."

"I did. I accept responsibility for that. Still, she goaded me into it. Why? That's the part I don't understand. Prophet, I need answers. I need to know what's actually going on here, not lies from the mouth of a Nation Builders goon." Edgar eyed Anvas with a weary stare, and Anvas shriveled.

"I wish I knew," Prophet said. "Do you always know why a person commits suicide? Are the reasons always apparent in hindsight?"

"You think Oracle used Edgar to kill herself?" Reis's eyes widened in surprise.

"It's one of many working theories I have," Prophet said. "Be that as it may, she is gone—and as impossible as it may be, I grieve for her."

"You're just a computer," Anvas protested. "You can't feel."

"In a conventional sense, of course not. But I've lived in the bodies of my people for so long, experiencing their lives, hopes and fears, grief, deaths, losses, and gains. I know what drives them all, and I can understand what they are feeling, even if I don't feel it myself, per se." Prophet stood in front of Anvas. "You've caused so much grief in the name of saving a country. Do you truly believe that a person who can only call upon their own life experiences and feelings is best to rule a country?"

"Humans should rule humans. You can't understand what it's like to live. How can you possibly make decisions for us?" Anver spat.

"Maybe that's what makes the difference," Prophet argued. "I only use data. My feelings and experiences don't factor into it at all. I analyze other countries' actions and take the best scenario for Anver. The most logical step forward, even if it's unpopular at the time. I can run the numbers. I can crunch the data. With Unification, I was even more powerful. Oracle allowed me even more data—the success of policies she implemented as an AI in charge of Kasyova and their failure rate, without the interference of human feelings and imperfect implementations coloring the information. Now, I have to rely more on the people who make up my government, but I have every faith that both the acting government of Kasyova and the Shadow Government of the Twin City-States will continue to do the best for their people."

"What about the nukes?" Anvas yelled. "Anver has stockpiled them in recent weeks."

"Of course. Nation Builders sends agents to destroy my people, destabilize my regime, and end Unification. Historical data has shown that amassing a nuclear deterrent is quite effective in similar circumstances. You don't have to worry, Anvas. You have nothing to fear as long as you don't try anything stupid. Nor do the Union States or the Eastern Federation—the data clearly shows mutually assured destruction for Anver if I make the first move. But merely having nuclear capabilities—and the location of Nation Builders headquarters on a ship in international waters—is enough to get you, the Union States, the Eastern Federation, and Nation Builders to leave, I assume. I'm only going to ask nicely this once, Tony Anvas. Leave the Twin City-States alone. Let the people have Unification and the peace they want—the peace that's logically best for their future."

"Zach?" Anvas turned to his partner. "This is bullshit. Don't tell me that you side with this lunatic dictator AI and its pretty words?"

"I'd side with it sooner than the man who planted a bomb inside his own daughter." Zach pushed Anvas away as he came in for an embrace. "I was never stupid enough to believe that what we had was love, but I never thought you'd stoop that low for control. Yet you'd stand here and try to tell me that you're more of a righteous ruler than Prophet?"

"I did what I had to do!" Anvas protested. "Mark my words; this computer may string together words that make sense, but what will you do when it 'logically' decides the human race is obsolete? I love you, Zach. Don't abandon me and Anver's independence now!"

Zach shook his head. He turned to Reis. "Am I to understand that the Shadow Government still has my daughter and that she is safe?"

"The bomb was removed successfully," Reis assured him. "When I left, she was stable and comfortable."

"Good. That's what I needed to hear." Zach lunged forward and grabbed the pistol from Reis's grip. He pointed it at Anvas and fired multiple times. Anvas crumpled, shock lining his features as he slumped into a spreading pool of blood. Zach pointed the gun at Reis as he backed away toward the elevator. "I'm sorry, but I can't be a part of this. I needed to be free of him, but I intend to return to Nation Builders and continue their mission."

"Zach, wait!" Reis yelled.

"Let him go," Prophet said. "I won't force him to agree with me. He has the right to follow whatever path he chooses."

"Logically, that's quite unsound," Edgar pointed out. "He may come back to destroy you at a future date."

"I have very little data to act upon regarding this situation," Prophet said. "Yet killing him for merely having a difference of opinion seems wrong. I will deal with Nation Builders in due course. It is more important for him to take my ultimatum back to them." The elevator doors slid shut, and Zach was hidden from view. "Edgar, I need your assistance. Please seize my secondary systems from Nation Builders' control. I will assist you with this task. We have a news bulletin to put out. The days of Anvas's fake news are over. It's time to once again sell Unification to the people."

Chapter Seventeen

REIS

Reis stood guard as Edgar worked through the night with Prophet, pulling back Prophet's secondary systems from the Nation Builders-backed Anvas Media Group and ending the propaganda broadcasts across the city. They took a brief nap, but something inside them was restless and eager to make a move. They were acutely aware and unsettled that Zach had escaped after shooting Anvas in cold blood. Reis's feelings on the subject were mixed. On the one hand, Anvas had stoked the flames of war and caused more deaths than Reis could count. On the other, he hadn't seemed like a raving, frothing ideologue but a man who was right in some ways and incredibly, painfully wrong in others. He'd believed himself to be the hero of his own story, bringing down the twin AIs to restore democracy—and Reis couldn't argue that democratic government wasn't a righteous goal. There was something unsettling about submitting to the rule of autocratic artificial intelligence.

Needing a break from the swirling thoughts in their head, they wrapped Anvas's body in a tarp and took him to the catering level, where a handy freezer still in operation would serve as a good temporary storage place until he could be buried. Reis peeled back the tarp to take one final look at a face they'd hated for so long and was disturbed to find they felt nothing. Vengeance was empty when it came down to it. The end of human life was simply that—the end. Anvas had died for what he believed, killed by the man who'd carried his child, yet Reis felt no satisfaction in that, only a kind of melancholy that lingered long after they'd left the freezer and returned to Edgar's side.

"Reis, are you okay?" Edgar asked, standing up from the stool he was propped on and stretching out.

Reis shrugged. "It's over, I guess. I feel like I should be happy, but…"

"Anver's truth bothers you?" Edgar asked.

"Yeah, a bit," Reis admitted. "We've discovered that our democratically elected government was never democratic in the first place."

"We were happy, though, weren't we?" Edgar offered. "Life in the Twin City-States was good before and between Anver's civil wars. Democracy is a grand idea but look at every major democracy in the world, Reis. All of them are riddled with corruption, greed, and bad decisions made to appease the court of public opinion and for the sake of re-election. Prophet solves all those problems."

"Prophet is benevolent—for now. But what if that

changes? Most democratic societies start well. Only after hundreds of years do the cracks begin to show. Prophet hasn't been around long enough yet to prove it's a good system."

"That's the one thing still troubling me," Edgar said. He drummed his fingers on the console to a tune Reis didn't recognize. "Oracle goaded me into killing her. Why? Did she suffer a system instability that I was unaware of? Or did logic dictate that her death was the best course of action? What if the same thing happens to Prophet? Or to us? Will we end this civil war only to be plunged into a new dark age?"

"You assume Oracle is dead," Prophet said. Her holographic form shimmered into view, that of a young woman in a dress sitting on the edge of the console. She swung her legs as if bored. "I assumed the same. It was a logically sound assessment to make. But now that I have my secondary systems back, I can see that my assessment was inaccurate."

"What do you mean?" Edgar asked. Reis lifted their head, their curiosity piqued. Was Oracle alive? But how? The virus the Shadow Government had created was designed to destroy every line of code, relentlessly hunting it down and erasing it. It would never have worked on Prophet since she'd put her code inside people as genetic information, but Oracle couldn't have done the same... could she?

"Did Oracle have a genetic information program as well with the Kasyovan recruits?" Reis asked.

"Nothing so well organized," Prophet stated. "I think

this counts more as an emergency backup situation." She clicked her fingers, and some grainy security footage appeared on the console.

Reis strode closer to get a better look, and their heart leaped out of their chest as they saw a makeshift morgue. Emily lay on an examination table, all but her face covered by a sheet.

Her eyes opened.

"That's not possible!" Edgar cried. "Oracle said she was going to die! I let our friend die, and there was nothing I could do to save her..."

"Is she even in there?" Reis asked. "Or is that Oracle inhabiting her body, now?" They needed answers, and fast, before the sickening hope spreading through their veins reached their face and became a smile.

"You have to understand that Emily Vos needed a lot of treatment. Her file includes details of an artificial heart, arm, and other systems. Nation Builders spent millions of dollars keeping her alive, hoping they could use her against you later. All Oracle did was download her vital files into the storage on Emily's system. She might have told you that Emily would die because she didn't know if she could do it without killing her, but it would seem that Emily is, at least for now, alive and well, along with Oracle. It seems like this may have been a mutually beneficial arrangement. A symbiosis of sorts."

"I can't believe it," Reis said. "Not until I see her with my own two eyes."

"So go," Edgar said. "I'm the one who was banished, not you. I still have work to do here, but someone needs to go to Emily and explain what's happening. I think it would come best from you, Reis."

Reis nodded. "I don't like leaving you here, but you're right. What should I do when I find her? Is it safe to download Oracle's files back into the mainframe underneath Kasyova, or are they still virus-ridden?"

Prophet shook her head, the hologram shimmering as she did so. "I'm cleaning them up as we speak, Reis. When you reach Kasyova, the system should initiate a transfer safely. I've sent drones and engineers to start working on the bridge; they should have some temporary solution set up for you to cross when you arrive. Any cars in the Pyramid's parking garage will be unlocked for you."

"What's the plan after that?" Edgar asked.

"Once Oracle is back online, we can return things to normal. While we've been here talking, the Union States and the Eastern Federation have announced a unilateral withdrawal from Anver, starting now. Nation Builders works fast. I've already opened up the Internet and television to access from the rest of the world, but it will take time to convince the factions to surrender their weapons."

"You don't intend to announce your presence here, do you?" Edgar asked.

"No. The illusion of democracy is required for the system to work. Without it, the people feel oppressed. You may not be comfortable with it, but the Twin City-States is a social experiment. Perhaps one day, we can tell the citizens they are ruled by artificial intelligence, but that time is not yet at hand."

*

Reis barely said goodbye to Edgar as they grabbed Edgar's pistol from his outstretched hand. A quick kiss sealed the deal, but it was hard to linger while Emily waited. They ran to the elevator and hit the button for the parking garage. Prophet obliged, speeding the express elevator up to the parking garage without concern for Reis's comfort. Reis fought against the motion sickness caused by traveling upwards so fast and reminded themselves that it was just a small thing to endure compared to all the hardships they'd come through thus far.

They emerged into a gloomy garage and took the first sedan they saw in the half-light, painted black like a Bureau car. Reis put their foot on the accelerator and sped into the low evening light. In the half-light, they saw helicopters and planes bearing the Union States and Eastern Federation flags taking off and flying overhead. The skies were busy, but the ground was quiet. The persistent rattle of gunfire was gone, and one or two people wandered onto the sidewalks. Reis saw people emerging from the subway stations as news spread from those who had media access that the war was coming to a close. Not that it would be that easy, Reis realized. It would take a long time to undo Nation Builders' propaganda that had set Anver's people against one another, and the lines drawn in the sand would likely endure for a long time. Prophet had her work cut out for her if she would restore Anver to its former glory.

But it was a start, and for the first time in a long time,

Reis's despair started to lift, pushed out of their body by the hope filling them up. Against the odds, Emily was alive. The foreign aggressors were gone. The city had something resembling a future again.

Reis slowed down as they came to the bridge uniting the two cities. A makeshift work crew had a crane in place and was lifting steel plates into place along the damaged sections of the bridge. It wouldn't be too stable, but it was no riskier than driving the railroad bridge had been. Reis waited, and to their delight, they could see on the far side that engineers from Kasyova were arriving to help. Before long, Reis was beckoned across. They took the drive slowly, trusting the steel wouldn't yield at this final juncture. It would be cruel to have come as far as they had, only to die here.

Reis reached the other side with a sigh of relief. They waved to the workers and drove toward the Senate building. They left the car in front as a confused police officer tried to tell Reis they couldn't park there. Reis pressed past him and took the steps up to the building two at a time. They burst through the front doors into the marble and granite vestibule. Hikaru Wynn waited there, but his face showed no signs of emotion. He led Reis into the stairwell, and they walked down in silence. He said nothing until they passed through the nondescript hidden door in the wall that led to the underground stairwell.

"When the lights came on, and the computers started booting up, we knew you'd somehow achieved the impossible and liberated Prophet from Anvas's hands," Wynn said. "Prophet took over our network shortly thereafter and explained she is now operating in alliance with you."

"Not quite," Reis admitted, "but she is free of Nation Builders' control and influence. Her secondary systems belong to her again. Zach fled, and Tony Anvas is dead. For real this time."

"My question is, why did you come back, Reis?" Wynn asked. "What possible purpose could you have here in Kasyova? Anver needs your help; the war isn't over just yet."

"Oracle is alive," Reis said. "She's inside Emily Vos. Her vital files are stored on the internal systems controlling Emily's artificial heart."

"Emily's dead, Reis."

"No. Somehow, she's not." Reis argued. "Take me to the morgue." Wynn gave them a cynical glance before shrugging and opening the door to the medical wing. Reis stepped through the door, and Wynn followed.

Emily stood wrapped in a hospital shift, doctors surrounding her with looks of horror on their faces.

"Step aside," Reis ordered, and the doctors backed away, opening a path for Reis to get close to Emily.

"Reis?" Emily asked. "I don't know what's going on... I'm so scared..."

"It's okay," Reis assured her. "I'll explain everything, but we must get you to a computer first."

"A computer?" Wynn asked.

"Prophet's cleaning the virus from Oracle's secondary systems. Hopefully, she can inhabit them again and leave Emily's body. With Oracle's assistance and repair,

Emily should be able to function by herself now." Reis took Emily by the arm and led her to a bank of computers along the wall. They helped her to sit at the console. The silence stretched out as the system booted to a blank screen.

"What now?" Wynn asked.

Emily smiled weakly. "I think I know," she said. "There's—there's someone else in here with me." She reached down and pulled a cable out from the computer. To Reis's surprise, she reached for the back of her neck and peeled up a flap of skin to reveal a port. She plugged the cable in and went limp, her body collapsing onto the console, which now displayed a progress bar.

"What the hell is going on?" Wynn asked.

"I think we need to wait and see," Reis replied, but they were as shaken as Wynn appeared. The Emily they'd known was a flesh-and-blood human, but she was also dead. Was this cyborg Emily, or some copy created by Nation Builders to infiltrate the Shadow Government? What if Emily was gone for good? What if she'd been dead all along?

The progress bar ticked along slowly—too slowly for Reis's liking. They perched against a metal table, trying not to look at Wynn, whose fearful glances back and forth between Emily and the console disconcerted them.

Finally, the progress meter finished. The computer completed booting, then Oracle shimmered into being before them. Reis moved to speak, but the blue-hued holographic woman standing before them hushed them with a finger on her lips.

"I know you have questions," Oracle said. "I can predict some of them. Yes, this is Emily Vos, not a clone, android, or facsimile. After her injuries at the wedding, Nation Builders saw an opportunity. They moved her to one of their state-of-the-art facilities, salvaging what they could from her body and fusing it with robotic implants. She is, in essence, a cyborg. The multitude of artificial systems in her body made it possible for me to store my data in her. Her brain is, however, hers. I can give her suggestions, but she is still the willful and bold Emily you knew. She registered as brain-dead because her biological systems are augmented with technology."

"Why is she unconscious?" Reis asked.

"She's rebooting. I had to make some changes, Reis. Nation Builders had some pretty nasty malware installed on her, keeping her in a coma on purpose so that she would be reliant on intensive medical care but also so that she could relay data back to them. I suspect they planned to wake her if they needed a sleeper agent, but your and Edgar's fortuitous arrival prevented that. I've deleted all spyware and malware from her systems, but they needed to restart. Her brain is just sleeping right now. She'll wake in a few minutes."

"Will she be okay?"

"If you mean will she be like she was before—well, I'd expect this experience will leave its scars, but there's no reason she won't, with care and support, go back to being the Emily you know and love. I have to give Nation Builders some credit; this is cutting-edge technology. Of course, those with the money to bankroll something like this must wield a large amount of money and influence. You may have won Anver back, but I suspect this isn't the last we'll hear from Nation Builders."

Reis nodded. Emily started to stir.

"Well, I'll leave you to your reunion," Oracle said. "I must interface with Prophet's systems and let her know I'm alive. From there, we have work to do. Thank you, Reis Asher. I'm sorry I used Edgar, but it was necessary. I'm glad my gambit paid off—you must love and trust him very much."

"I do," Reis said, their frown breaking into a smile. Oracle shimmered away as Emily sat up from the console and gazed at Reis. She blinked a couple of times and looked around.

"Did I fall asleep at my desk, Reis?"

"It's a little more complicated than that," Reis explained, "but I'll fill you in." They motioned to Wynn. "Let's get her to a bed."

They supported Emily as they left the room. Reis took one last look behind them at the computer bank that was just a minute part of Oracle's systems.

Oracle had saved Emily—booting Nation Builders out of her once and for all. She'd gone above and beyond to ensure Emily was her autonomous self again. Perhaps having artificial intelligence rule the Twin City-States wasn't a terrible idea after all.

Chapter Eighteen

EDGAR

The Loyalists and the Rebels were easier to bring to the table than Edgar had anticipated. Summer's group was instrumental in spreading the word that the Eastern Federation and the Union States were gone for good and much of the hearsay and news they'd received on the radio and in the streets was propaganda created by the two superpowers to justify their intervention in a proxy war.

It was a little too easy to cover up the fact that Anver and Kasyova were both ruled by artificial intelligence. Edgar felt more than a little guilty for perpetuating the lie that Kasyova was a democracy and they planned to return to democratic rule in Anver, but it was a necessary smokescreen. Both the Rebels and Loyalists wanted elections, and they would get them, even if Prophet and Oracle were manipulating the numbers behind the scenes. Only the fact that Prophet's scope was more limited than Edgar had initially realized kept him from being too eager to tell the truth. The AI dictated the country's direction, but the elected candidates still had roles that involved a lot more than just taking orders. They believed they were in control and that part of the illusion made the system work.

"It's time for you to go, Edgar," Prophet said. "I need to seal my chamber, and you need to focus on the human elements at play here. I can only manipulate people so much. I've brought the factions to the table, but you and Reis must convince them that laying down their arms is the best course of action."

"I still say I'm not the best one for the job. Reis is the people person, not me. Emily has a way of pulling things together. I'll just be an idiot sitting at a table, stammering over my words. I'm only fluent in programming languages."

"You're the calm one," Prophet explained. "You keep Reis balanced. You make a good team. The best."

"We do." Edgar had missed Reis in the busy weeks since they'd traveled to Kasyova. Despite being overwhelmed with the sheer amount of work involved in purging Prophet's secondary systems of Nation Builders' influence, the lack of Reis's presence felt like an imposed silence on his soul, and he couldn't wait to see them again.

"You shouldn't wait to marry. The world doesn't wait for anyone. Nation Builders is still out there. The immediate threat may be over, but nothing in this world is safe."

"Are you manipulating me?" Edgar asked. "You don't have to tell me to marry Reis. I already mean to, providing they're still willing after everything that's happened."

"You never betrayed Reis. They know that, now."

"I know they know. Everyone's safe. Emily's alive. Oracle's still functioning. We have hopes of forging lasting peace and returning to the way things were. It's more than I ever could have hoped for. Yet…some part of me believes they won't still want to marry me."

"That part is wrong." A familiar voice echoed through the chamber, and Edgar spun on his heel to see Reis barreling toward him. He caught Reis and spun them around, then set them down before Reis claimed their lips in a breathless kiss that felt like the first one all over again.

Except, this time, they weren't on the run. Nation Builders was licking their wounds. Maybe they'd have to deal with them eventually, but for now, he could relax for the first time in four years. He pulled away from Reis with reluctance. "We still have one more thing to do. We must seal the deal and get both sides to agree to abide by the elections."

"It's just a formality at this point," Reis said. "Breathe, Ed. Anverites want peace. It will be okay now that Nation Builders isn't meddling and the ceasefire has taken effect."

"I won't relax until it's all over. I might never relax again, come to think of it." He nestled his head on Reis's shoulder, forgetting for a moment that Prophet was in the room. "Nation Builders is still out there, and they won't forget that we are why their plans failed here."

"Then I'll protect you," Reis said. "They can send a

thousand people after you, and I'll shoot them all down to keep you safe." They smiled. "Let's leave Prophet to decide the future while we care for the present, okay?"

"Okay," Edgar said. With one last look at Prophet as she shimmered away, they entered the elevator for the last time. They'd all agreed that it wouldn't be a good idea for civilians like them to have access to the artificial intelligence beneath each city; the Shadow Government had also vacated the levels beneath the Kasyovan Senate Building. The rooms would be sealed and purged to a clean-room state, only to be opened in times of emergency when automatic maintenance wasn't enough.

It had to be lonely, in a sense, yet the two computer life forms had access to eyes and ears all over the Twin Cities, living vicariously through the people they ruled. Edgar realized he'd never be alone: Prophet and Oracle would always be watching, even if they couldn't directly intervene.

To this moment, Edgar still wondered if they'd pulled the strings more than they let on. Could Edgar and Reis have eluded the Killing Game by themselves? It seemed increasingly unlikely the more he considered it, yet he didn't want to ask. He liked believing that Reis had put everything on the line to save a stranger, that Emily had stuck to her beliefs and ousted Grady, and that Reis had earned their promotion to the Bureau. What would that mean for human achievement if Prophet and Oracle pulled all the strings?

No, some questions were better left unanswered.

*

The vestibule of the Pyramid milled with life when Edgar and Reis emerged. Work was well underway to restore the Glass Pyramid to its former glory. Gone was the shattered glass, the drones, and the dead bodies, replaced by construction workers who'd traded their guns for hammers now there was paid work to return to. The Kasyovan Government had officially bankrolled the restoration, but Edgar knew Prophet had earmarked the funds from an emergency foreign bank account she controlled. People all over the city were laying down weapons and getting back to normal life. The peace talks were largely a formality to set terms for legally ending the civil war in a way that suited everyone.

Reunification was on the horizon but hadn't been formally discussed. The Rebels were still set against it, and Prophet had decided it was better to reestablish a formal Anverite government before trying to merge with their neighbor once again. Even if Oracle and Prophet still ruled as joint systems, the outward sharing of civil and economic structures streamlined the number of things they had to oversee. From a practical standpoint, Unification had always made sense.

Edgar stopped momentarily, realizing Reis was no longer walking beside him. He turned to see Reis staring at the statue of Elias Torrell, Reis's father and the architect of Unification.

"Do you think—" Reis shook their head. "Unification. Was it even really his idea?"

Edgar placed his hand on Reis's shoulder and looked up at the statue with them. "It's possible the seed was already planted, but he dictated the specifics. He made it a reality. Along with his exit strategy. Or Anvas's, if you think of it that way. It's hard to attribute ownership of ideas. Everyone is inspired by everyone they meet and everything they experience. I imagine he wouldn't have been susceptible to any influence if he didn't already think it was a good idea, Reis."

"I don't even know if he was a good person. He loved me, yet he was the reason I became a child soldier."

"Nobody is purely a saint or a sinner," Edgar said. "I think even Tony Anvas had his reasons, and they weren't all wrapped up in world domination and profit." He thought of Anvas's admission that he'd loved Elias and wondered if Elias had ever felt the same way or if their romance had been an unrequited tragedy.

"What do you think Zach will do?" Reis asked.

"I can't say," Edgar responded. "He's a wild card. We may never see him again, but he may also become a thorn in our sides in years to come."

"I may someday have to put a bullet in him," Reis admitted. "I don't like that idea one bit."

"Neither do I," Edgar said, "but he has to make his own choices. Wynn's already found a suitable home for his daughter. She'll grow up never knowing her true origins."

"That's probably for the best," Reis said.

"Reis!" A voice echoed behind them. Reis spun around to see Summer wearing a skirt-suit. She smiled.

"Ready to make peace? I've got a bet on you having both sides come to an agreement within the day, so don't let me down."

"I'm not a miracle worker," Reis complained.

"Come on, Reis. Nobody wanted this war. Everyone will be glad to see it end. I know you can do this, just like your father did."

"Hopefully not," Reis said and walked out to the waiting limousine with Edgar in tow.

Chapter Nineteen

REIS

Reis flashed back to the press conference they'd held at the end of the Killing Game as they entered the formal conference room where the peace talks were slated. Loyalist and Rebel flags hung from the walls, along with the flag of Anver. Reis wished they'd been able to sneak the Twin City-States flag onto the wall, but they'd have to be content with the scarf they laid over their chair. They fussed with their red tie, wishing Edgar would hurry up and arrive already before they found themselves alone in an army of unfamiliar faces.

The door opened, and Hikaru Wynn stepped in. The Shadow Government's role in ending the conflict had been partially revealed in recent days, and Wynn was vying to keep his job as Bureau Director. There were many rumors about a possible presidential candidate, and Reis was happy to discover their name was not on the list. All they had to do was keep their head down here, and they could melt into civilian life with Edgar. Maybe they'd return to their job at the Bureau, but even that seemed too political for their tastes.

The delegates started to filter in and take their seats. Reis was relieved when Edgar sat beside them and squeezed their hand under the table. The room was soon filled with people Reis didn't know, faction leaders they'd not cared to learn the names of or know personally during the war. Anvas's successor in the Rebels, a woman named Aurora Young, stared across at Reis with a sneering glare. The Loyalist leader, Andrew Grey, looked curiously around with an open face. Summer stood as the leader of the Resistance. Alice Burnell and Rain Odell came as representatives of the Shadow Government, and Reis was relieved when Burnell started the introductions, seeming like she wanted to do most of the talking. Perhaps Reis was just here to fill the room. They started thinking of their wedding to Edgar; they'd made a few plans, but not many. What if they just tore on out of here and got married? Surely it wouldn't be that hard to find an official who could marry them?

But of course, that was the sticking point: Edgar didn't want the marriage certificate to read Anver or Kasyova, but the Twin City-States of Anver-Kasyova, and when Reis thought about it, they didn't, either. Reunification was their ultimate goal, and they couldn't call the job done until the final conflict was settled. Reis wouldn't feel right melting into the background of an independent Anver or Kasyova, thinking how much better they were together. Judging by the talks thus far, it seemed both sides might be happy to settle on leaving the question of

Reunification on the shelf.

The talks reached an impasse, and Burnell called a break. Delegates filed out, leaving Reis and Alice Burnell alone in the conference room.

"I haven't forgotten what you did to Edgar," Reis said. "I know you have hidden motives, and I'm watching you."

"I did what I did to Edgar out of loyalty to my country," Burnell replied. "I don't expect you to understand that—you are deeply loyal to a person, not a place. That's why the best politicians have no family which can be exploited or used as a weakness. You were a weak President with such an Achilles' heel. I still don't understand why Oracle chose you."

"Despite working for the Shadow Government, you have no desire for Reunification, do you?" Reis asked. "Even with everything you know...why?"

"It's simple. I think science and the arts don't belong together. The two cities have different needs, neither of which will be fully served by combining their organization. I worked for the Shadow Government because there was no Anver government to speak of, but things have changed. I might be your next President, Reis—so you'd be wise to drop your little grudge about me punishing someone I thought was a traitor."

"You tore out his fingernails. You put scars on Edgar's body that will never heal." Reis looked down at their own hands. They thought they were past this, but the bile that rose in their gut told them otherwise.

"I thought he had vital information that could make

or break our efforts against Nation Builders! Don't act like a child, Reis—you've killed people. You've done things you found distasteful because of your loyalty. I did what I had to, which is exactly what you've been doing all along. If you don't like what's happening here, Reis, speak up! You have a voice—or have you forgotten that?"

"I..." Reis sighed. "I hoped I could fade into the background and return to being ordinary. I wanted to ride into the sunset with Edgar. Maybe that's not possible after all."

"It's your choice, Reis Asher. If Reunification is something you truly believe in, then argue for it. The peace deal is settled. If you want to fulfill your father's legacy, now's the time. Or you can walk away. You don't have to be here. You can return to civilian life, marry the love of your life, and be remembered for saving him from the Killing Game. Despite our differences, I want you to know that I have Anver's best interests at heart, and I bear no ill will toward Kasyova. I'm no Tony Anvas. I have no desire to set Anver and Kasyova at odds."

Reis nodded and sat back down as the delegates filed back in. Edgar set two coffees down on the table, and Reis thanked him with a nod. They took the coffee cup in hand and studied Edgar as the discussions began anew. Contrary to what Reis had previously thought, Edgar listened intently to every word. His eyes followed every speaker in the room as they laid out their arguments and counterarguments. At one point, it seemed like he might speak himself, but the gentle parting of his lips and the slight sound that came out was silenced by a raucous Rebel who seemed to delight in shouting over everyone, and the room never seemed to realize that Edgar badly wanted to speak as they laid out the plans for an independent Anver without Kasyova.

Reis found themselves standing up, words forming somewhere between when they put their hands on the table and when their feet fully supported their weight.

"That's all well and good, but have you asked the people what they want? Have you given any thought at all as to whether the people of Anver and Kasyova might be interested in Reunification? All I hear here is 'I want' and 'Anver' but has anybody thought about the ramifications? Of families who will be divided across a border? Of policies almost identical that will have to be argued and decided twice in a vast exercise in redundancy, wasting money that could be better spent on funding the research that Anver is most known for?"

The room fell silent. All eyes fell on Reis, and they reddened, their cheeks glowing hot. Edgar nodded and smiled, giving them the strength to go on. Edgar had wanted to say this but hadn't been able to. Reis let their shields down and spoke from the heart, realizing it was Edgar's heart, too, that they'd always been united in their loyalty to the place they called home.

"Everybody thrived under the Twin City-States. It was the happiest, most productive time in both cities' history, marred only by Nation Builders' interference. Was there work that needed to be done to balance everything fairly? Sure, there was, because no system of government is perfect. No place is a utopia, but I was proud to live in the Twin City-States of Anver-Kasyova and call it my home. I fought and bled to save these cities, and I don't want to be forced to choose between them. I don't want my future husband to be forever considered a Kasyovan immigrant because both cities are his home! As they are for me." Reis realized they were leaning heavily on the table. They had a captive audience, held in thrall. "My father fought to create a perfect union of complementary states working toward a common goal. No other states in the world can claim to exist to advance one discipline or another: most of them exist in chaos, having lost their founding vision to time and corruption. But not the Twin City-States. We came together because science and technology influence the arts, and the arts influence science and technology. They may be separate disciplines, but they're not opposites. Both advance and enrich the human condition."

The room erupted into murmurs. Reis silenced them with a hand. A sense of purpose flowed through them, and they now knew why they'd come. It was more than Prophet and Oracle wanting them to: it was because they belonged here, arguing for the home that had given them their happiest years. "It's not enough to leave here with a peace treaty that splits us down the middle. We might agree now, but what's to keep us from engaging in war again down the line? My father knew that. He knew Unification was the best way to focus on our goals instead of our differences. He knew technology's sword could be powerful enough to destroy the world, so he wanted to temper Anver's hard edge with Kasyovan culture and music. He wanted to apply the Anverite sense of hard work and dedication to the laid-back Kasyovan culture. So that we might all live our best lives."

"What's to stop Kasyova from dominating us again in the future?" Burnell asked. "The old government was corrupt and funneled money away from Anver research projects into Kasyovan arts projects. That same corruption allowed Nation Builders to gain a foothold in the Senate and start the Killing Game that nearly killed both of you."

"We make sure that both nations have an equal number of representatives, unlike last time, when it was decided by population," Wynn suggested. "Reis isn't saying we can't change or tweak the system. It has to serve all the people of Anver-Kasyova, not just some. But it has to be a better solution than having two closed-off city-states in the same corner of the world just waiting to be invaded by a larger power. The tides may have turned in the Union States and the Eastern Federation, but that doesn't mean their greedy eyes won't stray here again."

Aurora Young's hard stare softened a little. "If we were to agree to Reunification, we would insist on a constitution outlining the rights of both Anverites and Kasyovans."

"That doesn't seem too much to ask," Andrew Grey replied. "A joint constitution would underline our mission for future generations."

Burnell started to sweat and shift in her seat, perhaps realizing she'd made a fatal mistake. Reis wondered if she'd lured them into talking in hopes of sinking the ship of Reunification once and for all, but if so, her plan had backfired. Both sides agreed, and Reis sat down as Grey and Young started deeper negotiations on what Reunification would look like.

Edgar's hand found Reis's under the table and squeezed. They looked at him to see pride, joy, and love reflected in those dark orbs and realized their work was done. The people would be okay now. They no longer needed Reis Asher to carry their father's torch. They could handle Reunification alone while Reis faded into a normal life with Edgar at their side.

The signed treaty looked very different from the one Burnell had been pushing for. Reis watched her leave, her proverbial tail between her legs as her political aspirations were shattered. All eyes seemed to settle on Reis, but Reis shook their head and guided them toward Wynn. He'd be a good President. The President everyone needed. A sensible person with a calm demeanor and loyalty to the end. Someone who knew the truth of Anver-Kasyova and respected it.

After the photo shoot, Reis took Edgar's hand and dragged him to the limousine. They sat back and breathed a long sigh of relief.

"It's over," Reis sighed.

"You were amazing," Edgar said. "What do you want to do now?"

"I want to go and see Emily," Reis replied, "and plan our wedding. It's about time I told the world how much I love you, Edgar Tobias."

Chapter Twenty

EDGAR

Edgar and Reis arrived at Emily's new apartment just as the home nurse left. They navigated the boxes in the hallway to find Emily sitting on a chair in the kitchen, analyzing the chaos around her with a look of despair that she snapped out of as soon as she noticed their presence.

"Hey," she said. "I thought you were never coming around at this rate."

"I'm sorry," Reis said. "We just came from the peace talks."

"Oh, yeah, those were today," Emily said absently. "I'm sorry. I've been having trouble remembering things since—since—"

"Since you died," Edgar said softly, breaking the tension with the truth. It was hard to say, but it felt necessary to acknowledge the gravity of the fact that Emily had been dead, even if science had brought her back.

"Right. It's a strange thing to say. I was gone. Blown to bits in an attack I barely remember. I can't even recall the face of the man I almost married."

"It's going to take time to put everything back to-gether," Reis assured, "but you have all the time in the world now." They pulled up a chair, sat amidst the boxes, and reached for Emily's hands. Edgar stood and watched as Reis took Emily's hands in theirs, squeezing her artificial fingers like they were comprised of flesh and bone. "The Twin City-States are getting back together. I argued for Reunification, and I won."

Emily's mouth upturned a little at the corners. It wasn't a full smile, but it was something. The beginning of a smile. The start of a new life. "I'm glad. It's good to know that everything I did wasn't futile."

"Far from it," Reis said. "If it wasn't for you, I doubt we'd still be alive. I know you don't remember much of it, but you saved us so many times..."

Emily nodded. "Are you going back to the Bureau, Reis?"

"I haven't decided," Reis said. "The Reunification Accords will be signed tomorrow. I want to marry Edgar after everything that's happened between us. I'll make my decision after that."

"The home nurse could barely bring herself to touch me," Emily said. "I can't blame her. Looking in the mirror is strange these days. I'm going to have to adjust."

"I can relate," Reis replied. "As you can see, I've been through some changes myself. They might be coming a little fast, however. I think...I'm going to pause hormone therapy for the time being."

Edgar swallowed. Reis had always seemed more

comfortable talking to Emily than him, but maybe that was a good thing. Reis always confided in her, and he didn't resent them having a true friend. Edgar reached forward, placed a supportive hand on Reis's shoulder, and squeezed gently to offer support.

"You have to do what's right for you," Emily said. "As do I. I want to go back to the Bureau as soon as I can. Just because Nation Builders is gone for now doesn't mean they'll stay that way. Hopefully, I can catch them before they infiltrate the entire organization next time." She closed her eyes. "Perhaps I just need to work. There's been so much to process, and so little of it has been good news." She looked up at Edgar. "Wynn came by and briefed me on everything. The courage you two have displayed... No country could ask for more loyal defenders."

"I did what I had to do out of personal loyalty more than political," Edgar said. "There was a point where I had to choose between my country and Reis's life, and I chose Reis."

"I heard," Emily said. "Both of you have earned a good rest. I'm also looking forward to your wedding since the last one I attended was...apparently not the greatest celebration."

"We're not having a big wedding," Reis pointed out. "That's why we're here. We're not going to be attending the Reunification Day parade and signing. We're planning to get married quietly while the world is distracted. We were hoping that you'd be there."

"I wouldn't miss it for the world," Emily said, "but what does a cyborg wear to a wedding?"

Reis fell silent, but Edgar knew what they were thinking—the same thing he was. Reis was too overcome to speak, so Edgar spoke his mind instead.

"You're not a cyborg. You're Emily," Edgar pointed out. "You could wear rags, and we wouldn't care. We're just happy you're here to see it. We thought our closest friend was gone forever."

A stray tear rolled down Emily's face, then another. She wiped them away with surprise. "So, I can still cry," she observed. "Good to know." She stood up and embraced Edgar and Reis in an awkward group hug, and they cried together, releasing all the pent-up sorrow, joy, and grief they'd held back for so long.

*

The courthouse was quiet, housing only a skeleton staff. Outside, the streets were alive with cheering as every Anver and Kasyovan citizen flooded the city square to witness the signing. Every television set was on in the waiting room, and Edgar smiled as Hikaru Wynn sat with the Kasyovan President and put his name to the Peace Accords and the Reunification Accords as well, signing Reunification into law, calling an election and declaring the day a national holiday. Edgar bit his lip, turning away from the television screen. It wouldn't do to cry now—he was saving that for the moment Reis kissed him.

The clerk ushered them into the courtroom. The judge—an elderly woman Edgar didn't recognize—smiled. "I've been waiting for you. Are you sure you want to forego the big ceremony? I think the Twin City-States will feel a little cheated to be deprived of their celebrity wedding," she pointed out. "The people could use something to celebrate after all the pain they've been through."

"No." Edgar closed his eyes. He'd been over this with a dozen other people. "We've given everything to Anver-Kasyova. This marriage is for us and us alone." He took Reis's hand, and Reis squeezed firmly, hardening his resolve to do this quietly. They'd had their time in the spotlight and were happy to leave it. This marriage was to be the start of a quiet, civilian life. They'd been to their home to find nothing but ashes. Reis had pulled their father's sniper rifle from the dirt only to throw it down again. They didn't need it anymore. Not the house, not the gun—none of it. This wedding was a new beginning for them, the chance they should have had after the Killing Game. They were done running from death. Now they could enjoy the bounties that life had to offer.

"Fair enough," the judge said. "Are the required witnesses present?"

Emily and Teon shuffled in, harried yet radiant. Emily wore a blue-and-gold dress that covered her from neck to toe. She still wasn't fully comfortable with her prosthetic body, but she was growing into it. Teon stood beside her, wearing a long red-and-gold body-hugging dress. A dozen gold bangles and bracelets covered each arm, and Edgar noticed their guitar rested against the bench. Of course—no Kasyovan would let a wedding go off without a song. He might have argued against it at one time, but now, he longed to hear his fathers' music almost as much as he wished they could be there.

"Sorry we're late," Teon mumbled. "Getting here wasn't easy with the crowds in the streets. I've heard it's a good day for a union." They smiled, and even Emily seemed to lose the flicker of sadness in her eyes.

"Thanks for coming," Edgar said. He drew in a deep breath and looked down at himself. The suit fit perfectly, but Reis wore theirs better. Edgar would never get over how good Reis looked in a suit. He noticed his own gnarled, healing fingers in the light. His fingernails grew back slowly, but he suspected they'd always look twisted and ugly. They all had scars from the things they'd seen and done.

Yet somehow, they'd made it here. To the altar. To marriage. To eternity together. Against all the odds, they'd survived. They'd won.

"We are gathered here today to witness the union of Reis Asher and Edgar Tobias," the judge said. Edgar knotted his fingers with Reis's, never wanting to let go. "Through hardship and pain, you have endured to reach this moment in time when two souls are bound together in legal matrimony. Edgar, do you promise to stay by Reis's side, for better for worse, for richer and for poorer, in sickness and in health, till death do you part?"

"I do," Edgar said without hesitation.

"Do you, Reis Asher, promise the same?"

"I do," Reis said. Edgar looked over at them, their eyes bright and sharp, and silently thanked the powers that be for bringing Reis into his life. He turned to Reis and took their other hand in his, gazing into their eyes.

"By the power invested in me by the Twin City-States of Anver-Kasyova, I declare you legally wedded."

Edgar picked Reis up and swung them around. He set them back on the ground before capturing their lips in a deep, passionate kiss. Edgar pulled away to see tears rolling down Reis's face, and he finally let his fall. They turned to face Emily and Teon, who were also crying. Teon had their guitar in hand and started to play. Edgar recognized the tune at once: "This Love of Ours," by none other than the Soulmates. Teon had sung this one originally, but Edgar's fathers had written it. It had been too long since he'd heard the familiar timbre of Teon's voice in song, their rich, deep, velveteen tones that grabbed the heart like no other. Edgar could almost feel the presence of his fathers, blessing this union. Would they be proud of his accomplishments, even if his talent wasn't for music?

No doubt they would. No doubt in the world.

Edgar and Reis walked hand in hand to the courtroom and out into the corridors. They let go of each other's hands, and Edgar felt the urge to run out into the sunshine and join the celebration.

They burst out of Anver's City Hall and onto the steps. The crowds turned away from the television screens as they were spotted, and soon the media was upon them. Teon caught up with them and showered them in confetti. They humored the video cameras and answered questions briefly before running to their limousine. Edgar shut the door with a sigh, and the driver darkened the windows, hiding them from view.

Edgar hoped it was the last they'd see of the public eye. He'd had enough of being visible for one lifetime.

Chapter Twenty-One

REIS

Reis stood at the window of their apartment in Kasyova, a stack of packed boxes behind them. They would miss the view, but their new home across the river in Anver was ready to move into. Anver was still quiet, but the city was starting to come back to life. Construction had sprung up everywhere after Reunification, and the best architects had traveled thousands of miles to make Anver rise from the ashes as the modern metropolis it was meant to be. Now, the first projects were being completed. Reis could see the lights illuminating the Glass Pyramid in the dying sunlight. The elections had gone without a hitch, and the people—or Prophet—had easily chosen Hikaru Wynn as their new President. A good choice, in Reis's opinion. Wynn would do right by the Twin City-States.

Edgar stood up from his laptop, clasping a cup of coffee. "Just wrapped that coding project. The customer's thrilled. You should see the tip he left me!"

"I'm glad. I'm sorry I've been so indecisive about my career." Reis pressed their hand up against the glass. "I wish I knew what I wanted to do. I thought it was my fate to hold a gun, but I realize that's what my father wanted for me. I don't want to fight anymore."

"Take your time," Edgar said. "Work is coming in hard and fast. I can support both of us for as long as you need."

"Thanks." Reis sighed. "Still. I need direction. It's okay to meander for a while, but eventually, I need something to aim toward. A goal. Purpose."

A knock on the door broke through the heavy conversation. Reis didn't give it a second thought as they headed to answer it. It was probably the moving company. Reis was surprised to see Teon, but glad at the same time. They didn't come over nearly often enough anymore.

"Teon!" Reis hugged them and ushered them inside before closing the door. "It's good to see you."

"Sorry I haven't been over too much lately," Teon apologized. "I've been a little busy with a project and need your help."

"My help?" Reis asked. "Not Edgar's?"

Teon shot Edgar a derisive look. "If I needed the tone deaf, I'd have hired a chorus of cats. No, Reis. I need a good pianist." Reis saw Edgar grin in the background and felt less guilty about the smile that flashed across their face. They put their hands up in protest before Teon could continue.

"I wouldn't call myself good, Teon. I enjoy playing

occasionally, but I'm not up to the standard you need for professional music."

"I'm just fucking around in the studio," Teon said. "It doesn't have to be anything incredible. I can't afford to hire session musicians, and besides, I want someone who might care about the album. It's a charity album to raise rebuilding costs for Anver's Museum of Science and Technology."

"I don't know..." Reis started.

"I think it sounds like fun," Edgar argued. "For the musically inclined, that is. I'd rather watch paint dry than sit in a studio, but you'd have fun, Reis. Why don't you give it a try?"

Reis let their mind wander for a moment. They recalled their mother playing the piano in the florist's shop long before their life was filled with pain, grief, and murder. They'd given up the piano to hold a gun, but now they'd given up the gun, perhaps it was time to take the piano back up again. Maybe they'd learn something with Teon at their side. It might just be harmless fun, but it might also lead Reis in a direction.

"Okay," Reis said. "I'd be honored to help, Teon."

"All right! I'll book some studio time for next week. You'd better start brushing up on your skills as soon as you move into your new home."

"Of course!" Reis said. When Teon left, they found themselves at their piano, dusting off the lid and lifting it to play a few notes. They were aware of Edgar's eyes on them and sat down to give him a mini concert. Inspiration flowed through their fingers like fire as old mental pathways opened up, long-forgotten talents pushing their way to the surface.

Long after dark, tiredness overcame them, and they stopped playing.

Edgar clapped. "I think you might have found the direction you're looking for. I'm just a tone-deaf cat with a biased opinion, but to me, it sounded like what my fathers called 'magic.'"

"You think so?" Reis asked.

"I do, Reis." Edgar's chestnut eyes were dark and serious. "Follow your path and see where it leads. Life is your song now, to sing as you choose, love."

Acknowledgements

Elizabeth Coldwell, for her editing and her patience!

About Reis Asher

Reis Asher (he/him) is a transmasculine author living in rural Pennsylvania with his husband and four cats. He loves video games, reading, technology, and of course, writing.

He enjoys shining a spotlight on queer characters and their adventures in a diverse range of worlds, from the fantastical to the everyday.

Catch him on Twitter where he's happy to interact.

Email

landale@me.com

Bluesky

@landale.bsky.social

Other NineStar books by this author

Killing Games Series

Killing Games

Killing Nightmares

CONNECT WITH NINESTAR PRESS

Website: NineStarPress.com

Facebook: NineStarPress

X: @ninestarpress

Instagram: NineStarPress

BlueSky: NineStarPress

Threads: @ninestarpress

www.ingramcontent.com/pod-product-compliance
Lightning Source LLC
Chambersburg PA
CBHW070539100726
47907CB00004B/1190